NOT LIKE Christmas AT ALL

A.R. ROSE

Edited By: The Cauldron Author Services

Proofread by: Virginia Tesi Carey

Character and Hospital art by: @magrnarts

OTHER TITLES BY A.R. ROSE

Ridgewood Series
*Between the Flames**
*Wicked Games We Play**
Marked By Cain

Standalones
Wreck Me
Only One Night
I Really Can't Stay

Twisted Heroes
Siren
A Captain So Callous and Cruel

With a Kiss
Sins of Sorrow
The Sinners
Sins of Bliss

Bridge Point Bears
Stealing Forever

**eBooks and paperbacks unpublished for rewrites. Original story available in audiobook.*

Authors Note

Not Like Christmas At All is a holiday read created for adults. Reader discretion is advised. Not Like Christmas At All contains content that may be triggering for some, as well as sexually explicit content.

Your mental health matters. For a full list of content warnings, please visit www.authorarrose.com/content-warnings.

To Veronica
This one's for you, my friend.

Chapter One

GENESIS

Two weeks until Christmas

"Paging Doctor Grumpy," the small voice of Mirabelle's announcement echoes over the hospital's speaker system, her innocent giggles following. "Doctor Grumpy! Where are you?"

"I said to call him Doctor Hottie!" My hand whips out to cover the mic, but my whisper-shout carries through the system. Stifling my laughter, I roll my eyes. My lips thin into an unamused line, and I mouth, "Really?"

"Ew, that's gross, he's old!" she shrieks, and it amplifies through the hospital because I still haven't flipped the off button.

"Wow, I see how it is. Pretty sure Doctor Hottie and I

are the same age." I could be wrong; I've actually never asked him how old he is, not like it matters. I'm at the beautiful, golden age where I could date him or his dad and be perfectly content.

Well, maybe not *his* dad in particular, but you know what I mean.

There's an audible click of plastic when I shut the PA system down. With the fakest stern look I can muster, I narrow my eyes at Mirabelle. "Way to blow our cover."

Laughing, she reverses her wheelchair, shaking her head. "That was all you, Nurse Tinsel-tits."

At twelve years old, her sass knows no bounds. I'm going to miss her when she gets discharged tomorrow morning. It was a real Christmas miracle *Doctor Hottie* was able to work his magic on her open leg fracture, but now it's time for my new friend to go home.

"Blowin' this popsicle stand in a couple hours, and she loses all sense of decency for her favorite nurse in the whole wide world. You know what? I'll remember that next time you're here." Which I hope is never. I adore all my patients, but I always hope to never see them again. At least not within these four very bleak, very sterile walls.

Her eyes widen a fraction. "I don't wanna come back." A visible shudder racks her petite frame, and I can tell I accidentally struck a chord.

Smoothing her hair, I boop her on the tip of her nose. "Don't worry, sugar plum. You're not invited back."

Mirabelle laughs and rolls her eyes. "Works for me."

"Come on, let's get you back to your room. You should've been in there twenty minutes ago! Your nurse is going to kill me!"

"*You're* my nurse."

I feign surprise, my hand pressing against my chest. "And the best nurse in this place!"

Pushing her wheelchair down the hall, I take Mirabelle back to her room which overlooks the super amazing—*insert sarcasm*—aesthetic of the boring parking lot.

It's no wonder she's been going out of her mind for the last three days. I've been trying to keep her company as much as I possibly can, but a girl's got to work. My patient list is a mile long.

It *is* the holidays after all. There's no shortage of accidents, and although I have a preference for working with kids, it's still my first year, and I'm stuck going where they tell me.

At least they let me wear pink scrubs every day.

That being said, I've spent every extra minute I have keeping Mirabelle entertained. Some patients you just connect with, and she and I bonded quickly. Although, I've learned two very interesting facts about my patient here that make my opinion of her slightly askew. She does *not* love the holly jolly season like I do—she thinks it's too cheerful.

Too.

Cheerful.

Is there even such a thing?

Mirabelle also said she prefers to celebrate Halloween!

Can you believe that?

Her argument? The candy is better.

The thought makes me laugh all over again—how freaking ridiculous.

She tilts her head back to look up at me. "What's so funny?"

"Oh, nothing," I singsong as we enter her room. "I'm just going to miss you. That's all."

"I'm going to miss you too, Nurse Gen."

This—this moment right here, knowing Mirabelle is on the road to a complete recovery and being discharged just in time to spend one of the most joyous times of the year with her family, is why I worked myself to the bone by pulling long days in nursing school, just to spend even longer hours at the hospital. Knowing I've done everything I can to care for this sweet girl brings me the greatest sense of peace and fulfillment.

When I started at the hospital, I was fresh-faced, doe-eyed, and excited for a new start.

My first day went off without a hitch, followed by my first week, but then a few days after *that*, the universe decided it was time for my luck to run out.

Late for my shift, I practically levitated through the hospital to get to a patient's room, only to turn a sharp corner and run directly into *him*.

Doctor Lincoln Stokes.

Surgeon.

Tall.

Handsome.

Respected.

Blond.

And I know what you're thinking. Blond? No way blonds are—

Stop it.

One look at him and you'll be ripping your panties from your body and slingshotting them just so he has something that belongs to you.

This is probably the part of the story where I should tell you a teensy, weensy, little problem with my good ol' pal Lincoln, though.

He hates me.

Okay, maybe hate is too strong of a word, but he certainly isn't my biggest fan.

You see, my best friend is dating his cousin, and while you may be thinking, *Genesis, that's a good thing!*

No, it's not.

No, it's not.

Because now, instead of seeing him in the hospital hierarchy as someone I need to be on my best behavior around, I take every opportunity I can just to mess with him. Hence the paging Doctor Hottie prank.

That may have been Mirabelle's idea...kind of.

Part of it.

Anyway, shockingly, Lincoln hasn't gotten me transferred—or fired—yet.

Yet.

I suspect it'll be coming at some point though, but it'll be a Christmas miracle if it doesn't.

An overly dramatic huff of annoyance sounds from my left, along with the squeak of tennis shoes hitting the shining linoleum floor of the cafeteria as the owner of said huff and shoes draws near.

When the scolding leaves his lips, the gruff tone pierces the quiet. "Those announcements were extremely inappropriate, Nurse Nikolaou." With his arms crossed over his chest, Linc—Doctor Stokes, since evidently we're being professional right now—comes to a stop next to my table with a scowl on his face.

I flip the page in my home decor magazine, *Flawless*

Design, not giving him the attention I know he's waiting for. Pretty sure this issue is from six years ago, but I liked the Christmas tree on the front of it and figured it was worth the flip. Plus, I had a feeling he'd come find me.

Not taking my eyes off the pages, I feign boredom. "I don't know what you're referring to, Doctor."

"Yes you do." He rips the magazine from my hands, forcing my gaze to move to his. "Paging Doctor Hottie? Really, Gen?"

"Oh, wow!" I press my hand to my chest. "How big your ego must be. There are many attractive doctors in this hospital, Lincoln. Who said you were the one being paged?"

"I—" He stops, closing his mouth as he processes what I just said. Blowing out an exasperated breath, he narrows his eyes at me. "You're a great nurse, Genesis, but you need to work on your professionalism."

"Relax, Ebenezer. It's the holidays! Have some fun. Pull the candy cane out of your butt—or don't." I lift my shoulders. "I don't judge."

"Jesus," he mutters, shaking his head.

With silent laughter, I pick my magazine back up and find where I left off before it was so *rudely* snatched from my hands.

Lincoln is a difficult one to read.

At the hospital, he always acts like I am the biggest

thorn in his side—a nuisance he doesn't want to deal with.

But when we're interacting in a social setting, with his cousin and my best friend, things are different.

Although he still doesn't act as if he likes me entirely, he definitely tolerates me more. We have a total frenemy situation going on, and frankly, I'm not sure how I feel about it.

I like him, which feels silly to even say as a grown woman, but I do.

My entire body and soul react when he's around, and it's a visceral feeling I can't explain, since we bicker more than we get along.

But right now—with him standing so close, his heavy gaze set on me—I can't help but squirm in my seat.

Flipping through the magazine a bit more, I ignore the silence between us and pretend to focus on the brightly lit Christmas trees and perfectly placed garland in the staged house glossing the pages.

Closing the cover, I place it down on the table, pick up my gingerbread latte, and take another sip. It's not very good, but the cafeteria staff gets a gold star for even attempting to create festive beverages.

Christmas is my absolute favorite holiday, and I'll

enjoy every morsel of this drink, even if it tastes like old dishwater.

Since I was a little girl, my parents always went above and beyond to make the holiday magic come alive for all of us. I have a big family—four sisters, three brothers, and my parents have two dogs, too. The Christmas season is a big deal in my family, but this year looks a little different for me.

Gone are the cold December nights spent cuddled under a snowman blanket, sipping peppermint hot cocoa, and watching Christmas movies at my parents' house with whoever's able to join. This year, it's been *me* who hasn't been there—my once cozy evenings are spent burning calories instead of consuming them, racing from patient to patient.

Of course, my family still includes me, whether it be through video chats or supplying me with this year's matching holiday gear—they make sure my holiday spirit is bright, even with my absence.

This year, my mom, sisters, and I bought matching red sequin hair bows with a candy cane in the center, and I've been wearing it practically every day at the hospital. It brings a smile to my face to see the patients' joyous faces when they see me decked out with extra holly jolly cheer.

"What's funny?" Lincoln grunts, reminding me of his presence, although really, how could I forget?

Stretching my silence, I finish the last sip of my mediocre latte and tap my foot in time to "Here Comes Santa Claus".

"Nothing." I scrunch my shoulders, then peek at the clock on the wall, noting I have about twenty minutes left of my break.

Briefly, our eyes meet as I stand, making me pause. I can feel Lincoln's gaze following me as I head to the trashcan to toss the empty cup. Walking out of the cafeteria, a smile tugs my lips knowing I've had the last word.

That will drive him crazy.

Heading back to the floor I'm working on today, I go into the nurses' lounge to spend my last few minutes of my break in solitude. Popping in an earbud, I call my best friend and drop onto the black leather couch that faces a large window, overlooking the busy freeway. Cars pass in a blur as I kick my feet up, settling in.

"Hey, Zee," I say as soon as her voice singsongs a greeting from the other end. "How's Pebbles?" My Great Dane is spoiled rotten whenever I'm on a long shift. I have a pet service who comes to walk her, but since Zee lives in my building, she will often head over a couple times a day to check on my girl.

I try to always return the favor by checking on her cat, Potato, whenever she's up in Julian at her boyfriend Miller's house.

Miller owns a Christmas tree lot, and she's been up there frequently, helping with the busy season.

"Pebbles is amazing, as always," she promises. "I actually brought her over to my place today, and Potato was excited to have a friend!"

Potato's never excited about *anything*, let alone seeing Pebbles. That cat has one mood—grumpy.

I laugh. "Yeah, right."

"How is your shift going?" she asks, the sound of a door closing in the background.

"Long. I'd much rather be baking Christmas cookies right now, but you know I'm on the crazy hours work grind these days."

"Totally get it. Well, I'm making Miller go caroling this weekend if you want to come with us," she offers, and I hear him groan in the background.

"Say less, I'll be there. Should I buy us matching sweaters?"

"What kind of question is that?"

"You're right, a foolish one. I'll place a pickup order and swing by the store after my shift. Any preference?"

"Nope!" she pops her p. "Whatever you think is cute, I'll think is cute."

"Love that for us. I'll get Miller one, too."

"Not necessary!" he yells from a distance.

Both Zee and I start laughing. Pulling the phone from where it's cradled against my shoulder, I check the time. "Alright, I gotta run, my break is just about over."

Before I hang up, I can't help but pull up my shopping app to see what I can add for a pickup order.

"Sounds good," Zee says in response. "I'll probably check on Pebbles one more time tonight."

"You don't have to, I have the pet service coming over to walk and feed her. She'll be fine, but thanks for checking on her earlier!"

HA! Bingo. I add three ugly sweaters to my cart, and man, do these take the spiced cake on ugliness.

"Anytime! You know I'm always happy to help. I'll see you tomorrow! Get home safely."

"See you tomorrow!" Hanging up the phone, I finish placing my order, then toss it onto the couch next to me, rolling my neck from side to side.

I've been up for nearly twenty-four hours, and I'm absolutely exhausted, but there's still a few hours left on my shift. I should have slept while I could, but sleeping while at work takes some getting used to.

Dragging my eyes to the window, I notice the clouds darkening as they roll in. What started out as a sunny day here in San Diego, now looks as dreary and bleak as an afternoon in Washington. A shiver runs through me as I think about living somewhere that constantly rains—no thank you!

With that being said, San Diego hasn't had rain in a while, though, at least in the last few weeks. I wonder if we're about to be hit with a winter storm.

I *really* hope that's not the case considering Christmas is in two weeks, but I guess we'll just have to wait and see.

I guess it'd be kind of fun to have a white Christmas for once...

Chapter Two

GENESIS

Peppermint or gingerbread?

I stare at the creamer options in my refrigerator. The pot of coffee gurgles and spurts as I decide what flavor I want my morning lifeline to be. Finally, I opt for peppermint.

My eyes burn, having pushed myself past the brink of exhaustion. I only slept six hours when I got home, and while that's an adequate night's sleep for some people, I need a full eight.

When my steaming cup of coffee is in my hand with the sweet and sharp notes of peppermint wafting into the air, I sit in the oversized chair by the window. I pay an exuberant amount in rent for this gorgeous view of Mission Bay, overlooking the sparkling water and sandy bayside beach, so I try to enjoy it as much as I can.

While I'm lost in thought, my phone vibrates in the pocket of my robe. Carefully, I shift my cup into my left hand and pull it out, seeing Zee's name lighting up the screen.

> Have anyone special you want to bring caroling?

Scrunching my nose, my fingers fly over the screen as I respond.

> Did you put too much Baileys in your coffee this morning? Why would you think I have someone to bring?

The only romantic relationships I have are with Christmas flavors I can add to my coffee—peppermint, gingerbread, toasted marshmallow—and I love them all equally.

> I don't know, just checking! You know how Miller and I had a whirlwind romance. An overnight love affair can happen to you, too.

> You're the exception, not the rule, Miss Holly North.

Holly North was the pseudonym Zee created last Christmas when she decided to join a dating app to go on a few dates over the holidays. One of her dates was a cozy Christmas Eve dinner, with none other than *Doctor Hottie*, which led to her meeting the love of her life, Lincoln's cousin, Miller.

> Oh my gosh!

> You should do what I did!

I purse my lips, trying to decode what my best friend is encouraging me to do. Then, the lightbulb turns on at the same moment another text appears on my screen.

> You should set up a SparksFly account.

> No way.

With what time? I barely have time to eat and sleep, let alone *date*.

> Yes! It could be so good.

> YOUR CHRISTMAS NAME COULD BE NOELLE WINTERS

Okay, stop. That's actually kind of cute.
And believable.

Noelle Winters could totally be someone's real name...then I realize where my thoughts have carried me. My fingers fly furiously over the keyboard, texting a response.

> And do what exactly? I don't have time to go on holidates, Zee!

> No, but you have time to get a little holidick.

I chose the wrong time to take a drink of coffee, practically spitting it out as I laugh out loud.

My phone vibrates again.

> Just do it. Nothing has to come of it, but it could be fun.

A huff of annoyance deflates my lungs, and for a few seconds, I simply stare at the message. Zee's never been overly interested in my love life—never to the point of pushing me to meet someone. She knows I've been focused on myself and building my career.

Which brings me to my next question.

> Where is this coming from?

Three dots show up at the bottom of our message, then disappear. It happens twice, then her text finally comes through.

> Lincoln's bringing a date to caroling.

The words across my screen cause a lump to form in my throat.

Lincoln's bringing a date.

Does that bother me?

Yeah, it does. But it shouldn't.

> I can take a raincheck if you want it to be a double date.

> NO! That wasn't what I was insinuating.
> I just wanted to give you a heads-up.
> Please still come.

> Okay.

My answer is short, but irritation rushes through me. Not only because Lincoln's bringing a date, but because Zee thinks I need to bring someone now. Why? I can handle seeing Lincoln on a date.

I have a crush, not an unyielding love for the guy.

Tossing my phone to the side, I return my full attention to my coffee, sipping the foam from the top. My chest tightens as I mull over Zee's texts, replaying them in my mind. She's never felt the need to tell me about Lincoln's plans before, and I haven't clued her in on how I've been feeling. She knows I think he's attractive and I love to tease him while we're at work, but I've never flat out told her my attraction to him is more than just physical.

After another few sips of my coffee, I pick my phone back up and open up the App Store, searching for SparksFly.

Should I download it?

If Zee hadn't taken the leap of faith last year, she would have never met Miller.

But then again, I'm not actively looking for anyone. I have no time for a partner at this stage in my life.

A hookup, however...

Why not?

Within seconds, the app is downloaded, open to the sign up screen, and ready for me to input my information.

Hesitantly, I fill out the questionnaire.

```
Noelle Winters
Twenty-eight
San Diego
Bio: Can you light up my life like a
Christmas tree?
Interests: Spending time with family,
the holidays, my dog. Not looking for
anything serious or long-term.
```

Uploading my favorite photo of me from last Christmas—me looking at my parents' Christmas tree, my wild, curly raven-colored hair swept back with a red velvet bow—I clench my jaw, wavering for a moment, before clicking submit.

There.

Done.

The screen immediately refreshes, opening to the profile of a somewhat attractive twenty-three-year-old, but I swipe on by. My palms start to sweat while I peruse a handful of men the app wants to match me with, all of which are handsome, and surprisingly, seem to be successful.

A few do catch my eye, and I swipe to confirm my interest, but once we've been paired, I close out of the screen, not wanting to be the first to send a message. I'm not ready for that next step—maybe I shouldn't have created an account to begin with.

My phone hits the couch with a soft thud as I toss it aside, also abandoning my now empty mug on the coffee table, to go get dressed.

As miserable as it'll be, I need to go to Fashion Valley Mall today and shop for gifts for my sisters. Leave it to their bougie asses to have expensive taste, forcing me to shop at the upscale mall I try to avoid.

When I enter my bedroom, Pebbles groans, stretching on her oversized plush bed. Pushing open the curtains, I let the daylight assault my poor sleeping beauty.

"Wakey, wakey, eggs and bakey!" I singsong, bending down to scratch behind her ears.

With another stretch, her long legs stiffen before she rolls over quickly, jolting her giant, horse-like body upright with a big yawn.

The plush duvet on my bed looks cozy and inviting, a symphony of down feathers practically begging me to crawl under them.

As though she hears the call of their comfort too, Pebbles takes a singular leap onto it and curls herself back into a ball.

"Alright, fine. Ten minutes, *max*, okay?" I relent, crawling up beside my girl. She exhales a deep sigh when my arm drapes across her, content to have morning snuggles. Her eyes shut as she falls asleep despite having just woken up, and before I know it, I'm asleep too.

Message received

SUBJECT: NAUGHTY OR NICE?

HEY NOELLE,
ARE YOU ON THE NAUGHTY LIST?
WOULD YOU LIKE TO BE?

-TRAVIS

——

Message received

SUBJECT: DAMN, GIRL.

DO I TURN ON...YOUR LIGHTS? BECAUSE
YOU TURN ME ON.

LET ME KNOW,
CHAD

———

Message received

SUBJECT: JUST LIKE SANTA

I'M IN TOWN FOR THE WEEKEND AND
LOOKING FOR A HO, HO, HO...

XX - KYLE

———

Throwing my phone across the room, not caring where it lands, I listen to the resounding thud as it connects with what I assume is my dresser, but can't be too sure because I've already squeezed my eyes shut in regret.

Why did I let Zee talk me into creating a dating profile? And better yet, why did I go through with it?

The too bright clock on my bedside table tells me it's past three in the afternoon. I never intended on taking a four hour nap, but apparently my body forced me into recouping from the long hours I pulled at the hospital.

And it's only going to get worse.

According to the weather app that sent an alert earlier, San Diego is about to get hit with a storm...and judging by the social media I scrolled through before tackling the SparksFly notifications, people are already in a frenzy.

The ding from another notification reverberates through the room from where my phone lies on the floor.

"Ugh." Pushing to my feet, I swipe it from the carpet as I pass by, heading to the bathroom.

Ignoring the alert from SparksFly, I set it on the bathroom counter and prep my toothbrush, shoving it into my mouth. The intense mint flavor assaults my tastebuds as I brush my teeth, and I turn back to look through the door leading to my bedroom. Pebbles is still lying on my bed, sprawled out, snoring, without a care in the world.

Goofy dog.

My phone pings again, and with the toothbrush still hanging out of my mouth, I reach for it, opening the app that's going to get deleted promptly after I read the new messages.

Message received

SUBJECT: ONLY HERE FOR THE WEEKEND

HI NOELLE,
I'M ONLY IN TOWN FOR THE NEXT FEW
DAYS FOR A SPORTS MEDICINE
TRAINING, AND WOULD LOVE TO SPEND
THE SMALL POCKETS OF FREE TIME I
HAVE WITH A BEAUTIFUL WOMAN. ANY
INTEREST IN DINNER WHILE I'M HERE?
SATURDAY?

OH, MY NAME'S LIAM, BY THE WAY. LIAM
WAGGONER. I SHOULD HAVE LED WITH
THAT.

———

Clicking on his profile picture, I nearly drop my phone with how handsome this man is. Short light brown hair and piercing honey brown eyes with a smile that could kill.

Liam Waggoner.

His bio says he's a team doctor for the Bridge Point Bears, which brings the sports medicine training full circle.

Dinner this weekend...

Shit, I already made plans to go caroling with Zee, Miller, and Lincoln.

And his date.

With a deep frown, I look back down at Liam's picture, then click back into the messages.

Hesitating, my fingers hover the screen, not sure if I should answer, or what I should even say. But before I know it, my response has been sent.

SUBJECT: ONLY HERE FOR THE
WEEKEND

HOW DO YOU FEEL ABOUT CAROLING?

———

I close out of the app, not expecting to get a response right away. Spitting, I rinse my toothbrush, then lean over the faucet to rinse my mouth with water.

Before I've even had the chance to put my toothbrush back in the holder, an alert lights up my screen.

Message received

SUBJECT: ONLY HERE FOR THE
WEEKEND

WELL, I CAN'T QUITE CARRY A TUNE,
BUT I'M ALWAYS UP FOR AN
ADVENTURE. WHAT DID YOU HAVE IN
MIND?

———

A spike of giddiness trickles through my bloodstream, and I bite down on my lip to try and suppress the smile naturally floating to my lips.

SUBJECT: ONLY HERE FOR THE
WEEKEND

I PROMISED SOME FRIENDS WE WOULD
GO CAROLING.

Message received

SUBJECT: ONLY HERE FOR THE
WEEKEND

WILL YOU LET ME BUY YOU DINNER
AFTER?

——

Resisting the urge to kick my feet and squeal, I carry my phone into my bedroom and sit down on the edge of my bed.

SUBJECT: ONLY HERE FOR THE
WEEKEND

LET'S SEE HOW CAROLING GOES FIRST.
ANY INTEREST IN GRABBING HOT
CHOCOLATE BEFORE WE SING OUR
HEARTS OUT? AT PERK UP? 6:30?

Message received

SUBJECT: ONLY HERE FOR THE
WEEKEND

THAT SOUNDS PERFECT. I'LL SEE YOU
THEN, NOELLE.

——

Exiting the app, I toggle over to my phone's search engine and input his name. Sure enough, the top website is the homepage to the Bridge Point Bears.

Liam Waggoner *is,* in fact, who he says he is.

A mild wave of guilt hits me square in the chest knowing I'm lying about my name, but it's not too late to be truthful when we're face to face.

I'll feel him out. See if he gives good guy vibes, or if he's a secret serial killer.

Either way, I feel a rush of endorphins knowing I'll have a date for caroling. Maybe it'll help combat the jealousy I know I'll feel seeing Lincoln with a date of his own.

Chapter Three

GENESIS

There's an incessant beat in my chest, thundering like it may explode at any second, as I pull open the door to Perk Up a couple days later. Work has been insane—that winter storm hit intensely, rain coming down in sideways sheets that didn't let up for several long, dreary days. Coffee with Liam, after getting to know each other better over text, is a welcome distraction.

Stepping inside, the warmth from the shop drifts around me like an embrace as my eyes scan around, looking for the man I'm supposed to meet.

I was hoping I'd be early so I wouldn't have to be the one to seek him out, but it seems like my punctuality is no match for his. As I look across the room, I easily find Liam Waggoner, team doctor for the freaking Bears, already sitting at a table with two steaming to-go-mugs in front of him.

I read no less than eight articles about him and the team, and I'm a little ashamed to admit it makes me even more nervous. It feels like I'm about to go on a date with a celebrity.

As though he can sense me, he looks up, eyes immediately finding mine, and a bright grin appears across his face. Like a gentleman, he stands as I approach the table.

"Hi," he greets, his eyes roving my body unabashedly. "Wow, Noelle. You're even more beautiful in person."

Not wanting to continue the ruse of a fake name throughout our whole date, I shake my head. "Actually, my real name is Genesis. Gen, for short."

"Ah." He nods slowly, still smiling wide. "I figured it was either a fake name, or your parents were just super into Christmas."

"Well, the latter isn't too far off, but I'm afraid my real name isn't as festive."

He rounds the table, pulling out my chair for me. "Well, Genesis is a beautiful name. I hope you don't mind" –he raises his to-go mug– "I grabbed your hot chocolate already."

There's a flicker of concern in my gut as I take my

seat, looking down at the drink he easily could have spiked. I don't know him, and my instincts tell me to refuse the drink, but my manners tell me—

"Oh, shit. I wasn't thinking." Liam picks the drink up, never making it back to his chair. "Let me order you another so you can see them make it."

My eyes snap to his in surprise. "Oh, that's—"

"No," he cuts me off again. "I have a sister, and I would never want her to accept a drink from someone without seeing it made. It doesn't matter if it's alcohol or hot chocolate."

Wow. "Thank you."

Liam squeezes my shoulder. "No problem."

Walking over to the counter, he tosses the hot cocoa into the trash as he passes it by. I'm still stunned, but grateful, because I would have sat awkwardly with it in front of me otherwise. The gesture speaks volumes to his character, and I relax into my seat further, shrugging off my jacket.

The ugly Christmas sweater I put on is sweltering, but I know once we start caroling I'll be cold, which is why I wore the extra layer. There's always a chill in my bones, which does nothing to combat my blanket buying addiction.

From over my shoulder, I watch as Liam reorders my drink, then turns back to give me a small smile. He waits patiently for the barista to remake it, then saunters over to me once it's in his hands.

"Here you go." He places it in front of me, then rounds the table back to his seat. "So, caroling, huh?" Leaning back, he crosses his arms casually over his chest.

"It was either invite you or decline your offer, and I'm sorry to say I was far too intrigued by your profession to say no."

"That's fair. Most people are enamored by the job title." Liam's face falls slightly, his eyebrows knitting together.

A nerve was struck, and as fascinated as I am by what he does, his occupation isn't what makes him *him*. "Well, it's pretty cool. But you can tell me about it later, if you want. Tell me about *you*."

Instantly, his spirit seems to lift.

Guilt laces with curiosity—do most women only care about his social status? Do they use him to get to the Bears players, or something? A crack fractures my heart thinking about it.

"Where'd you grow up?" I ask, starting with something basic.

"Well, my father was in the military, so all over the world, really. But California is where we stayed the longest, and where I eventually made my home."

For the next hour, Liam and I sip on our hot cocoas and get to know each other better, and while I'm not sure I feel a rush of endorphins in his presence, I sense he's one of the good ones.

He has to be. He agreed to go caroling on our first date.

Speaking of which, it's almost time...

By the time Liam and I leave Perk Up to head to the neighborhood we're meeting everyone at to carol, the temperature outside becomes frigid, and by frigid I mean California cold which is around forty-eight degrees.

Pulling up along a residential curb, I cut my engine, turning off my headlights. Liam's headlights blind me through my mirror as he pulls behind my car. They go dark, then we both exit our cars at the same time. He greets me with a warm smile and steps closer, waiting as I engage the lock.

"It got chilly," he comments, shoving his hands in his pockets.

Up ahead, I see Zee, Miller, Lincoln, and his date waiting for us by a large camphor tree. My car door's slam echoes through the quiet street.

"Yeah, it did." I rub my hands over my jacket-clad arms, smiling at my friends. Zee sees me and waves excitedly.

Liam tips his head in the direction of where everyone stands. "Is that the caroling crew?"

Nodding, I loop my arm through his, and we start walking their way. "Sure is! Zee—the girl in the red jacket—and Miller, her boyfriend, are great, you'll love them."

"What about the other couple?"

My heart sinks at the word *couple*. "That's Lincoln, Miller's cousin, and his date. I haven't met her yet."

The words die on my tongue as we take our final steps and are face to face with the group.

"You made it!" Zee squeals, tossing her arms around my neck. She squeezes tightly, and whispers, "He's freaking cute!"

As I laugh, she pulls away and extends her hand in Liam's direction, shaking it with enthusiasm. "Hi, I'm Zee. This is Miller"—she gestures to each person as she introduces them—"Lincoln, and Ashlee."

Miller gives me a side hug. "Good to see you." Turning to Liam, he shakes his hand too. "Nice to meet you, man."

"Likewise." Liam grins, then says to the whole group, "You know, I'm really not much of a singer, so this is a first for me, but I'm looking forward to it."

"Don't worry, we'll just hide behind the women and let them do their thing," Miller reassures him.

I watch their exchange, relaxing a little, but from across the group, I feel a heavy stare on me. A rush of nerves filters through, and as I lift my gaze, it collides with Lincoln's.

The impenetrable look reflected back steals the air from my lungs, my heart suddenly pounding.

I'm the first to break our stare, and I immediately wish I hadn't as my line of sight falls to where Lincoln holds his date—Ashlee's—hand, their fingers laced together.

Blowing out a shaky breath, I return my attention back to Liam, looping my arm back through his. He smiles down at me briefly as he continues his conversation with Miller.

We carol through the neighborhood for the next forty-five minutes, and despite this being one of my favorite holiday activities, my mind is elsewhere. I can't concentrate on enjoying the feeling, and instead, I'm nervous—hyperaware of the men as they stand behind us, adding their baritone sporadically through the songs as they remember the lyrics. We visited every house on both sides of the street, only skipping a few who weren't home. When the last lyric is delivered at the last house, we all head back to our cars with smiles, frozen noses, and the promise to do this again next year.

After we part ways, Liam walks me back to my car, opening my driver's side door like a gentleman.

"I had a great time tonight, Gen. Thank you for inviting me." His hand reaches up, brushing a piece of my curly hair that's fallen out of place. "Do you have any interest in coming back to my hotel for a nightcap? Alcoholic, or non—your choice."

Glittering with hope, Liam's hand lingers on the top of the door, holding the metal as I stand between the car and the door.

There's a split second of hesitancy on my part, but ultimately, I shake my head. "Thank you for such a lovely evening tonight, but I better head home."

"That's okay." Holding his arms open, I step closer to him and wrap mine around his middle. "I'm in town for a couple more days. If there's any downtime, I'd love to see you if you're free too."

"That sounds perfect," I agree, pulling from his embrace and dipping down to get into my car. "Thank you again, Liam. It was so great to meet you."

Engaging my seatbelt, I smile up at him before turning on my car.

"Merry Christmas, Gen." He knocks his fist against my roof twice before shutting my door for me. The windshield begins to defrost as he tucks his hands into his jacket pockets and heads back to his car.

Part of me wants to stop him—invite him to my place. But I bite my tongue. Watching him through the side mirror, he turns his headlights on and lets his car idle, the silhouette of him not moving until I realize he's being a gentleman, waiting for me to leave first. There's another moment of hesitancy, wondering if maybe I should step outside of my comfort zone and pursue this man further, before I put my car into drive and speed off in the direction of home.

Chapter Four

GENESIS

I wake up with a headache that makes me want to crack my skull in half. Or maybe it's already cracked in half with how it's pounding.

By the time I fell asleep last night, my mind had volleyed the thought of two men back and forth more times than I should probably admit. I kept thinking about Liam and how sweet he'd been. On paper, he's a catch. Heck, in person he's a catch too. There should be more attraction to him on my part, but I can't help but to feel closed off to the idea of him.

He'd texted me shortly after parting ways to make sure I got home safely. The gesture was sweet, and not completely unexpected considering how he immediately sprung into action with the drink situation earlier.

We'd texted for a while before he finally ended the

conversation, needing to wake up early for his conference.

Once my phone was plugged in, I turned over on my side and began to stew in silence.

Memories of how Lincoln stared at me when he saw me with Liam—the unreadable look on his face. Was it a look of indifference? Or annoyance?

Logically, I know Lincoln feels nothing for me. He tolerates me, at best. I'm the woman he can't seem to shake at work, or in his personal life. And despite my attraction to him, and my preference for driving him insane while at the hospital, I know that's where our relationship—*friendship*—ends.

At times, the word friendship can be interpreted in different manners, too.

Not *really* friends.

Best friends.

Friends with *benefits*.

God, I wish.

We're hardly friends at all.

It took a while before my brain settled down and I was able to fall asleep, and now that I'm awake, headache in tow, my thoughts have picked up right where they left off.

Patting my nightstand until my fingers reach my phone, I pull it off the charger and squint to look at it, pulling up Zee's contact to do some recon.

Gen: Caroling was fun. What'd everyone think of Liam?

My bed shakes as Pebbles rolls over, her long limbs sticking straight in the air as she settles on her back.

LOVED him! Miller and I both agree you need to date him.

I know better than to ask what Lincoln thinks of him, but it crosses my mind. Luckily, I don't need to.

It seemed like Lincoln's date didn't go as well as yours did. Ashlee had the personality of a sardine. He was in a pissy mood the second we were ready to carol.

Interesting...

I can't date him, he lives in Northern California.

So there's these really great methods of transportation called airplanes...

I'm not a long distance kind of gal.

We stop texting, but I know it won't be the end of our conversation.

Forcing myself to get out of bed, I pad over to my window, pushing open the curtains. The sky is dark despite it being mid-morning, storm clouds covering every square inch of blue. Spinning on my heel, I walk back over and pick up my phone, toggling over to the weather app.

One hundred percent chance of rain, and is that... snow?

That can't be right.

In disbelief, I open a different weather app on my phone, convinced the first one is wrong, but sure enough, small little snowflakes illustrate this app as well.

I'll believe it when I see it.

With a stretch, I throw my phone back onto my bed, accidentally hitting Pebbles in the paw when I do. She groans in protest.

"Sorry, Princess Pebbles, I didn't mean to!" The baby voice is thick as I look at my dog from across the room, my lower lip worried as though she completely understands my words and mannerisms. Nevertheless, my apology seems to work, and she makes herself comfortable again.

When I'm dressed in my favorite pair of yoga pants and oversized Christmas sweatshirt, with fuzzy socks tugged up to my knees and my hair piled on top of my head in a messy bun, I leave the room with only one ambition: coffee.

The rest of my apartment is cool, and I shiver, making a pit stop to crank up the heater before finally indulging in a steaming hot cup of Christmas cheer. The gingerbread creamer today has me moaning a happy hum as I take a sip and melt onto my couch.

It's too quiet in my house as I sit, looking out the window again and taking in my view of San Diego.

I love living here. There's so much to do year-round, and so many opportunities at every turn.

For a fleeting moment, I'd thought about leaving—uprooting myself, and starting over somewhere fresh, especially when I finished nursing school—but I couldn't picture myself anywhere else.

My mug is almost empty when my phone starts beeping repeatedly from my bedroom, notifications dinging as my phone receives text after text.

Part of me wants to ignore it and stay unplugged for a little longer, but a sinking feeling in my gut spurs me to stand.

I've barely made it back through the threshold of my bedroom when the phone begins to ring.

The name of the hospital's chief, Rebecca Grady, flashes across my screen.

This can't be good.

Doctor Grady only calls when there's a staffing emergency, *especially* when she knows it's someone's day off.

"Hey, Chief!" I keep my tone chipper, hoping my instincts are off and I'm not being called in. She *could* be calling about anything—a paperwork error, a question... wanting recommendations for a book. The sky's the limit, honestly, but I know I'm too optimistic. I should be preparing myself for the worst-case scenario.

No more days off for me.

"Hey, Genesis," she greets bleakly. I resist the urge to sigh. "I'm going to need you to be on call from now until when your shift starts tomorrow. You know I wouldn't request this unless it was necessary, but with the winter storm rolling in, I want us to be all hands on deck and prepared for anything. It's been a long time since snow's been forecasted for San Diego."

"Do you actually think we'll get snow?" It's been decades, so naturally, I find it hard to believe.

"Hard to tell, but I've been watching all the weather reports and checking the apps and they all say the same. Regardless, the rain should be hitting within the hour, and you know people in California are awful at driving in the rain. We're going to need the extra manpower."

"You're right about that. I completely understand." Although as I say the words, my heart sinks. I'm supposed to have family dinner tonight, and I haven't had the chance to see my whole family in weeks. I really don't want to miss it, or be called out halfway, but I know when it comes to my job, I have to pay my dues and earn seniority.

"Thanks, Gen. I knew I could count on you. Try to enjoy your day, just keep your phone on you."

"Will do! And let's hope for the sun!"

She laughs, then hangs up without another word.

Groaning, I sink back down onto my bed and let my eyes shut. Ten minutes to sit, then I'll prepare everything I need for work, so I'm ready to go if I get called in. Last time this happened, I had to be there within an hour.

Let's hope that doesn't happen again.

"Why the hell do you always look like you just stepped off Santa's sleigh?" Lincoln eyes me with a look of distaste as I fly out of the elevator. He's standing at the nurses' station, talking to Olivia, a nurse who's around my age. I'm in my scrub pants, but still rocking my light up holiday sweater after realizing I forgot the long-sleeve shirt I like to layer under my scrub top. Thankfully, I keep a few extra in my locker at work, which is where I'm heading now.

Breezing past him, I shout from over my shoulder, "I don't need your sass right now, Doctor Stokes. I've got a mom at nine centimeters waiting for another nurse."

The nurses' locker room is empty when I push my way through the heavy door, but I notice the sound of it shutting takes a few seconds longer than it should. Ignoring the footsteps behind me as they draw closer, I enter my combination, disengaging the lock quickly and easily locating my white long-sleeve.

The exasperated huff behind me lets me know exactly who's followed me in here. "It's unprofessional for patients to see you in plain clothes."

"I thought my clothes were too festive? Now they're plain?" I quip, slamming the locker closed. Spinning the lock, I quirk a brow. "Are you going to just stand here while I change, or?"

Lincoln sends me a glare. "First off, I'm a doctor. You don't have anything I haven't seen before, Genesis—"

I feign a gasp. "Nurse Nikolaou, Doctor. I thought we were keeping things professional."

"Nurse Nikolaou," he repeats through gritted teeth. "Second, don't flatter yourself."

Turning, he faces the lockers opposite of mine, folding his arms over his chest.

I silently chuckle and pull my sweater overhead. He doesn't need to know I have a tank top underneath.

Tugging the long-sleeve on, followed by my scrub top, I dress quickly, then lean against the lockers. "Was there something you needed, Doctor?"

He sneaks a glance—well, a glare—over his shoulder at me. When he sees I'm dressed, he rolls his eyes and faces me again. "Yeah, I..." His voice trails off and another crease divots between his brows. "You know what? Never mind."

"Aw, Lincoln, don't get all flustered!" I call out to him as he hustles away. But he surprises me by stopping, although he doesn't turn around. And I'm not sure why I'm compelled to keep poking the bear, but I do. "I think you just need a little holiday cheer in your life. Want me to go get you a sweater?"

My heart rate increases as I wait for his response, but it doesn't come. Instead, he shakes his head and leaves me standing in the locker room alone.

Ten minutes later, I'm brushing sweaty tendrils of golden-hued hair off my patient's forehead with one hand, while she squeezes the life out of my other. "You've got this, Mama! Breathe through it. Doctor Newhall should be here any second."

Incoherent cries fly from her as she squeezes her eyes shut. "I need to push!"

I send a nervous glance to a nurse with far more experience than me. She nods once. Turning my attention back to the patient, I gently squeeze her hand. "Okay, let's have a baby then! I want you to push when I tell you to. Are you ready?"

Adrenaline courses through my veins, excitement overtaking me. Although I'm not entirely sure what area I want to specialize in, I'm never disappointed when the floater pool brings me up to labor and delivery.

With another squeeze of the mom's hand, I count backward from three and settle in to help bring a little miracle into the world.

Chapter Five

GENESIS

Every floor is quiet, the awful fluorescent lights a bit lower, and the hustle and bustle of the day has become slower, more leisurely paced. Emergencies are at a minimum too, at least for now. It's the middle of the night—the time I cherish most. When I'm able to process and think, and take a second to breathe.

Some nights, anyway.

It's past two A.M. by the time I finally have a moment to fuel my body and can take a quiet moment for myself. Grabbing some extra snacks from my locker, I ride the elevator down to the ground level and head into the hospital's cafeteria. Light whispers fill the room as I enter the staff area, helping myself to a few of the healthier snack options the hospital keeps on hand for us, since meal service is long past closed. I grab a meat and cheese snack pack from the refrigerated vending machine to pair with my apple and granola bar, then look for a place to relax for a while.

Some nurses I've only met a few times in passing sit at a table nearby, and across the room, I spot Lincoln sitting at a table for two next to the window overlooking the parking lot.

A sigh reverberates through my chest as I draw nearer to him, not sure if he'll even want my company, but I'm not really in the mood to be alone.

Today was rough, and I'm fearful the silence of my chaotic thoughts will open up my mind to the grief I've felt several times this shift.

"Can I join you?" My voice is small, a sense of timidness slipping through me, and I'm not sure why.

I've *never*, and I truly mean never with every sense of the word, been concerned over interactions with a man, and I can't figure out for the life of me why I want the approval of *this* man so badly.

I tell myself it's because of Zee, that I want this aspect of her relationship with Miller—the piece of it where everyone they care for can do things together—to be as easy as possible, but deep down, I know that's not the *real* reason.

I've never cared much about finding a boyfriend, or the thought of settling down. Sure, companionship is great, but it hasn't been a priority in my life, and I still feel like it isn't. My family, my career, *those* are my priorities...but Lincoln has me curious.

I'm a firm believer in everything happens for a reason and have no doubt in my mind the reason my best friend was compelled to go on all of those holidates last year was to meet the love of her life. But I can't help but wonder what the reason for her bringing Lincoln into *my* life was.

She didn't have to introduce us.

Although I would have met him regardless, since we now work together.

Lincoln grunts in response, and I take that as my green light to pull out the chair across from him. The cool bite of the metal seeps through my scrubs and sends a small chill down my spine. Arranging my snacks in front of me, I ask, "Hungry?"

"No, I'm good." His gruff voice is doused in exhaustion, and I notice the dark circles under his eyes.

The plastic on my cheese whines as I rip it open. "When do you get to go home?"

"Not soon enough," he grumbles, placing his phone down on the table. "You?"

"Tomorrow afternoon. But not for long."

"Working the holiday?"

"Unfortunately." My throat clogs with emotion

again, like it does every time I think about working on Christmas.

This will be the first holiday in my entire twenty-eight years on this planet where I won't get to spend it with my family. I knew the realities of this career when I decided to take the leap, but it still doesn't make it any easier. "Hopefully I'll be able to see them on the twenty-sixth though."

"I'm sure it will be pretty quiet around here. Why do you like Christmas so much, anyway? You're practically a walking billboard for the North Pole."

"It's always been my favorite time of year." A smile ghosts my lips as I think about the warmth the holiday embodies. "What's not to like?"

Vacantly, Lincoln looks past my shoulder across the room before answering. "Everything. It's just another day, Genesis."

My heart stutters and feels like it falls to the depths of my stomach at his obvious distaste toward Christmas. "What's your family doing for the holidays? Do you get to spend it with them?"

He casts a glance back at me before refocusing on whatever he's looking at over my shoulder. I'm not sure what else to say in follow up to such a simple question, so I stay quiet and take another bite of my cheese stick.

A sigh I can only describe as annoyed pushes past

his lips. But as much as I'm clearly a thorn in his side, he's a thorn in mine, too. "Our holidays are always small. I head up to my parents' house in Julian, Miller comes over, and we just hang out and relax. Mom makes a huge spread of food, and we watch football."

There's a twinge of jealousy that makes my heart beat faster. He gets to enjoy time with his family this year, and he's taking it for granted. Maybe that's not a fair assumption, but based on his tone, it's a very educated guess. "Exactly what the holidays should be about. Family. Good food."

"Always is. This year, Zee will be there."

"She told me! I'm so happy she has your family now." My best friend tragically lost her family about a year and a half ago in a car accident. Her brother was driving their parents home when they were hit by a drunk driver.

"Yeah, she's great. My cousin's a lucky man." He glances at me briefly, then flips his phone absentmindedly between his fingers.

"So why do you hate Christmas so much then? It sounds like they're great."

"I'm just not a fan," he answers without hesitation, with a sense of finality in his statement.

Every other question swirling in my mind dies on my tongue.

Behind me, metal scrapes across the linoleum flooring, but I can't tear my gaze from Lincoln's. The lack of expression on his face has the question screaming in my mind: why does he hate Christmas so dang much?

But it's past two in the morning, and I can't bring myself to push the issue. Unable to suppress it any longer, I let out a yawn, and our conversation goes quiet.

Suddenly feeling a little awkward in Lincoln's presence, my thoughts run rampant, and my incessant need to know everything practically drives me to the brink of insanity. Turning my full attention over to my snacks, I push them around, hyperaware of every movement he makes. The air's thick with tension, and I realize I'm having a hard time deciphering what kind of tension it may be.

He surprises me when he asks, "Does your family exchange gifts?"

My eyes snap to his. With a smile, I nod. "We're big gift givers! But there're so many of us, we rotate how we give each year."

"What do you mean?" He leans forward with his elbow on the table, resting his chin against the heel of his hand.

My cheeks heat under his gaze. "Some years we do Secret Santa, or white elephant, but we've also done a gag gift exchange, which was a lot of fun."

"What's this year?"

Sinking my teeth into my bottom lip, I suppress a laugh. "Have you ever seen the social media videos with those giant plastic-wrapped balls people have to break into with oven mitts on?"

"Uh, not that I'm aware of?" His eyebrows furrow with confusion.

"So, you take a giant package or two of plastic wrap and wrap gifts within it as you roll it into a ball—the tighter, the better, with as many gifts as you can get in there. Then, whoever's participating stands around something like a table or the kitchen counter, and one person has the ball, while the person next to them has a pair of dice. When it's your turn with the ball, you try to rip or unroll your way to the gifts inside while you're wearing oven mitts, and the person next to you is trying as quickly as possible to roll doubles. As soon as they do, they steal the ball from you, put the oven mitts on, and try to break into it before the next person rolls doubles. It can be pretty intense, but it is so much fun. You get to keep whatever gifts you're able to get out of it."

His lips purse, and he crosses his arms over his chest, casually leaning back in his chair. "What kind of gifts do you even put in a ball of plastic?"

"Anything you want, that's the beauty of it! This year we all had to go buy twenty dollars' worth of things, plus two five dollar gift cards. I grabbed easy, small essentials like hair ties, lip balm, and mini bottles of hand sanitizer. I know one of my brothers said he picked up a couple small bottles of alcohol, and extra gift cards. I'm looking forward to seeing what everyone else came up with!"

"I'm intrigued," Lincoln announces, but I'm skeptical if he actually is. Honestly, he looks a little bored after my word vomit of the game's overview.

"You should be," I tell him matter-of-factly. "I'll have to mention it to Zee, so maybe one year you guys can play that at Christmas, too."

"Maybe."

Another silence plagues our table, and I check my watch. Only fifteen minutes have passed.

Deciding it's time for me to head back upstairs, I gather the rest of my snacks and stand. "Well, I'm going to try to lie down for a bit before rounds. Thanks for letting me sit."

"Yeah, no problem."

Where this shift at work has drained my energy, Lincoln has drained the Christmas cheer right out of me with his overall frigid demeanor toward the holiday. Never mind he never seems to smile when he's around me but always seems friendly and happy when other people are around.

I can't figure him out, but as I walk away from the table we just shared, I can't help but fantasize what it would be like to have the other side of him. Smiling. *Laughing.* The Lincoln Zee tells me about and is so fond of. I don't get that side of him, just passing glimpses every so often.

But if there's one thing I know for sure, it's that his obvious passiveness about the holiday I hold so dear to my heart has me feeling like the only logical next step is to avoid him until after Christmas.

Petty, maybe, but I want to enjoy the most wonderful time of year, and when Dr. Lincoln Stokes is in my presence lately, it feels akin to hanging out with Scrooge.

So as the doors to the cafeteria swing closed behind me, I promise myself to do exactly that. Christmas is in three days—Lincoln isn't working the holiday, and I'm off tomorrow. This should be easy. Really, I only have to stay away from Lincoln for a few more hours.

Operation avoid the grump and recharge my Christmas battery is now in progress.

Chapter Six

GENESIS

Less than twenty-four hours later, I'm sitting cross-legged on my couch, crying into a bowl of peppermint ice cream while on a video call with my mom. How pathetic am I? I don't know why I'm being hit with an onslaught of emotions over having to work on my favorite holiday, but even I can recognize I'm taking it to the extreme.

I have no rationality when it comes to this. At least I'm aware of my idiocy though, right?

It's seriously stupid.

Picking at a peppermint chunk with my spoon, I sigh. "I shouldn't be this emotional over having to go to work, right?"

"It's okay, Gennie, your feelings are valid." My mom's comforting voice slips around me as though she is here, embracing me while she strokes my hair. "However, this is the career you picked, and you were born for this job. Christmas can be celebrated any day of the year—in fact, we have no problem waiting until the twenty-sixth to uphold our traditions. The date on the calendar makes no difference in significance."

"I know, Mom. Rationally, I *know* I need to stop whining. I'm acting like a child."

My mom chuckles. "You are, but I understand, my girl. Be happy you have a wonderful place to work with patients who value you as their nurse. Plus, you have so much celebrating ahead of you! With us, and then with your first holiday party at the hospital. Are you looking forward to it?"

Honestly, there's a part of me that doesn't even want to go. But I don't tell my mother that.

The hospital's annual Christmas party is being held in a ballroom at a swanky hotel in downtown San Diego. Based on the chatter I've heard from other nurses, it's an amazing event. The board truly goes out of their way to give a show of appreciation for the staff who are able to attend. They host it the week between Christmas and New Year's, rather than trying to cram it in before Christmas, and I've been told they do a great job at rotating who is scheduled to work that day.

"I don't know, I may n—"

"Don't you dare finish that sentence. You *are* going." My sister, Briar, walks into the frame, cutting me off mid-word as she finishes it for me. Her beautiful face appears next to my mom's on the small screen. "You've already picked out the dress, and you have the heels. All you need is a blowout and a little makeup, and you're party ready."

"Oh, is that all I need?" I sass back, knowing damn well she's correct but refusing to acknowledge it. We went shopping a few weeks ago and picked out a beautiful chocolate-brown tulle dress I'm utterly obsessed with.

"Yes! That, and the confidence to walk in there like the badass bitch you are."

A badass bitch walking in *alone*.

That's the other thing I don't love about the holiday party—I don't have a date. Liam and I have already cut ties, quickly realizing a long distance flirtation doesn't suit either of us. We left things on great terms, with promises to reach out if either of us were ever in the other's vicinity. But I have no plans of visiting Northern California anytime soon, so while it's a lovely notion, it's not a realistic one.

"We'll see. Maybe I'll spend the evening wrapped in my fluffy robe, curled up on the couch with a bowl of popcorn, instead. Pebbles is the perfect date for a movie night."

"Don't you dare, Genesis! Your days of relaxation are saved for your days off work."

"Technically, I'm not working if I'm going to the holiday party." I raise my brows in defiance.

"You know what I mean." Briar rolls her eyes, and I can see Mom's attention flit between me and my sister, on standby to diffuse a potential argument.

I laugh, ready to shut this conversation down. My sister and I get along great until we don't, then it's like we're teenagers all over again.

We stare at each other through the screen for several seconds before she relents and sighs deeply. "Do you want to go to a movie later? There's a new romcom out I've been wanting to see."

"As much as it pains me to say, I'm going to pass. I can feel the exhaustion deep in the marrow of my bones. All I want to do is go back to sleep."

"Understandable. Well, we'll see you tomorrow for sure. Are we sticking to tradition?"

"Why would we break it?" A jolt of anxiety spikes at the thought of another piece of my holiday ripped away.

"I don't know! You can't come on Christmas, so I just wanted to make sure our Christmas Eve tradition was still on."

"That shouldn't even be a question in your mind, B."

"I am making lobster bisque this year," Mom butts in. Picking up the phone, she stands and starts to walk away from Briar. "And Auntie dropped off a fresh loaf of her sourdough this morning."

"Then we're going to caravan around and look at Christmas lights while drinking peppermint hot chocolate, right?" God, the more I speak, the more I sound like a child.

"Yes, Gennie, of course that is the plan. We will head to Candy Cane Lane, then go over to Kringle Court."

Her words put me at ease. "Good. I like that plan."

"It's been the same plan your entire life."

"And that's why I like it. Nothing wrong with that."

"You're right, my love, there is nothing wrong with that," she coos.

"All right, I've got to run, Mom. My duvet is calling my name again. Love you guys." I blow a kiss into the phone.

"We love you. See you tomorrow."

Then, with a final wave, I hang up.

No sooner do I set my phone down does Pebbles come running from the kitchen, her bowl of dog food long past devoured. Taking a leap, she hits the couch next to me and lays her head in my lap.

She's jonesin' for my ice cream, and although her puppy dog eyes are hard to resist, I boop her on the nose instead of sharing. "No, no. Peppermint is bad for doggos."

Doing my best to ignore her, I push the play button to turn on the movie I was watching, even though I know for a fact I won't make it another fifteen minutes with the way my eyelids are feeling like they weigh thirty pounds each. But I am determined to at least make it to eight o'clock.

Abandoning my now empty ice cream bowl onto the coffee table, I pull my blanket up to my chest, snuggling in with my dog-shaped body pillow. Although it's pretty bony and wiggly if you ask me—and it snores.

But none of that matters because soon I'm falling asleep, listening to the rhythmic breathing of my dog as I settle in on my cozy couch. I should get up and go to bed, but I can't bring myself to care, let alone move, and soon my dreams are of happy Christmas memories.

"So tell us about this baseball player," my dad prods after swallowing a large spoonful of his steaming hot soup.

I nearly choke on mine.

"Mom!" My spoon clatters against the oversized

bowl in front of me as I set it down, sending a glare across the table.

I've been waiting for this all night though. From the moment I walked through the door of my parents' house, I could feel his stare following me around, and I caught him suppressing a grin more than once—a tell-tale sign he was sitting on some information and was bursting at the seams to word vomit it.

My dad is a terrible secret keeper.

Mom shrugs. "You know I tell your father everything."

"Yes, but in this case, there was nothing to tell," I insist, then turn my attention to him to extinguish his excitement. "It was nothing, Dad. We went on one date. He was very nice, and he entertained me by going caroling with my friends, but we're not even talking anymore. Also, he wasn't a baseball player! He was the team's doctor."

"That's even better!" His hands flail in front of him. "Why are you letting such a successful man get away?"

"Who's to say he's successful?"

"He's the private doctor of a major league baseball team. If you don't count that as a success, I don't know what success looks like to you."

My fingertips press into my temples as I lean my

elbows on the table. "Like I said, he was very kind, but it would never have worked out. He lives up north."

"You young people have no concept of time apart. A little long distance can be healthy. That's what they did back in the day. Tons of successful relationships were long distance when the men went off to war."

Oh God, here we go again.

"Leave her alone, Peter!" Mom smacks his chest. "Gen does not need a man to make her happy or define her success. She will eventually meet someone and settle down when the time is right."

"Maybe he's just not the right type of doctor for Gen." Fern, my younger sister, shrugs her shoulders. Her lips purse with a mischievous smile.

Immediately, I shake my head in her direction and narrow my eyes. Fern is the only person I've told everything to. She's a year and a half younger than me, and we've always been close. However, if she doesn't shut her mouth right now, she is going to be *very* close to the ground instead.

Possibly six feet beneath it.

"Oh," my older brother Elliott butts in. "Pray tell, little sis."

"Did you meet someone at the hospital?" My mom's eyes sparkle with curiosity.

"You met someone and you didn't tell me?" Briar

squeals at the same time my middle sister, Parker, scolds, "How are you going to meet a hot doctor and say nothing? I feel betrayed."

From across the table, two of my brothers start busting up laughing.

"Well, tell us about him," my father urges.

I bury my head in my hands.

What in the actual snowball effect is happening right now?

With a groan, I push the heels of my hands into my eye sockets, willing myself to disappear.

"For God's sake, everyone, calm down. I didn't meet anyone," I finally snap. Ripping my hands from my eyes, my vision blurs, but quickly clears to the sight of far too many curious eyes on me.

"Liar," Fern mumbles under her breath, and since she's sitting right next to me, I hurl my elbow into her side.

She grunts. "Ow, Gen, what the hell?"

"Yeah, what the hell?"

"All right, my children," Mom's melodic, yet authoritative voice raises through our bickering. "Settle down. It's Christmas Eve, and you're acting like heathens. If Gen says there is no one, then there is no one. Be respectful—all of you!"

"Thank you, Mom." Crossing my arms over my chest, I glare at my siblings.

With a soft chuckle, Mom stands and begins to stack empty soup bowls, holding them between her hands carefully, then walks into the kitchen. Seconds later, the sound of running water from the faucet fills the air. I'm still staring daggers at my siblings when we all hear a gasp, followed by a clatter of ceramic hitting the metal basin.

Our father is on his feet faster than I can blink.

"It's snowing!" she squeals, excitement bubbling out of her as she claps her hands together, pressing up on her tiptoes for a better look out the window overlooking the backyard. "And the snow is sticking!"

"This is San Diego; we don't get snow." My youngest brother scratches the top of his head, walking over to the sliding glass door to see for himself.

Pushing it open, the freezing air flows in, and we're all able to catch sight of the snow coating the artificial grass. "Well, damn. I guess I'm the liar of this house now. Look at this shit!"

Following him out onto the back patio, my arms instinctively wrap around my middle for warmth. In each hand, he forms a small snowball, then chucks one in my direction and the other in Elliott's.

As the crisp little snowball connects with my shoulder, it's like every member of the Nikolaou household has been transported back in time to when all of us were kids and my parents took us to see the snow for the very first time up in Julian.

But we're not *in* Julian this time, and it's been sixty-five years since San Diego's last snowstorm—a rarity that just doesn't happen this close to the ocean, when our weather is practically perfect year-round.

But as my younger sister slips her hand into mine and gives it a squeeze, I know we're all thinking the exact same thing: it's our first white Christmas.

And if I have to miss Christmas Day with my family, at least I get to be here on Christmas Eve to experience this with them.

Chapter Seven

GENESIS

A yawn hits me as I step off the elevator. The early morning sun casts a warm glow through the hallway as I approach the nurses' locker room, and I'm greeted by a veteran nurse with a warm smile as she pushes open the door for us both. "Hey, Nurse Nikolaou! Don't you look spritely."

Despite being bummed about spending the holiday at the hospital, I've come in with my Christmas cheer in full force. A red sequin bow, this one sporting a Santa hat in the center, holds my hair in a festive messy bun, and I'm wearing my favorite pair of candy cane socks, which match my pink scrubs perfectly. I'm in labor and delivery again today and excited about the possibility of delivering an extra special gift today.

"Merry Christmas to you, Nurse Edwin! Are you

working the full day?" Spinning the lock on my locker, it opens easily, and I shove my purse inside, then tug my cardigan from my shoulders. It's freezing outside, and as I remove the warm layer of clothing, I realize inside isn't much better.

The snow hasn't let up since I left my parents' last night, and according to the weather forecast, it's expected to get worse before it gets better. Although I'll be inside all day, I'm still riding Cloud Nine that I got to experience the first few hours of San Diego's white Christmas with my family. It's almost more than I could've asked for, and it made me feel so much better about not spending today with them.

"I'm afraid you're stuck with me all day, dear." Nurse Edwin gives me a warm smile and pats me on the shoulder. "I don't mind it though. My family is back east, and no one wants to travel to spend the holidays with this old bird. Not with the cost of flights these days."

"Why don't you go to them?"

She gives me a tight lip smile. "Fear of flying."

"I get it. I'm not much of a traveler myself. Well, why don't we try to make today as fun and festive as we possibly can?"

Taking a seat on the couch, she kicks her feet up on the small coffee table, closing her eyes as she leans back, settling in. "That's the spirit, my dear. I can't wait to see what you come up with."

"I won't let you down." The quiet clink of metal resounds as I push my locker shut, then leave the room with a slight pep in my step, feeling giddy from the idea of making today as warm and vibrant as possible. No one said we had to spend Christmas in the hospital without having a little fun, right?

Aside from the tree and pitiful looking garland in the lobby, there isn't an ounce of Christmas magic to make the patients feel like today is a day worth celebrating. I can't imagine there aren't decorations hiding in a closet somewhere in this hospital, and it's now my personal mission this morning to try to find them.

Pushing the door a little too excitedly, it swings open, and I ungracefully collide into Doctor DeAngelo, slamming against his firm chest. It scares both of us, and as I gasp, he takes a quick, wide step backward.

"Oh my gosh, sir! I'm so sorry!"

"In a hurry, Nurse Nikolaou?"

Running my hands down the front of my scrubs, I laugh nervously. "Um, sort of. Do you know where I could locate some holiday decor?"

"*Here*?" He arches a brow in interest. "No. Aside from the large tree in the lobby, I've never seen this place decorated."

Heart sinking in disappointment, he confirms what I already suspected—this place has always had a lack of festivity.

"Thank you, Doctor. So sorry for slamming into you."

"Not a problem, Nurse Nikolaou." His watch beeps, drawing his attention to his wrist. He's already lost in thought when he mutters, "Merry Christmas," and continues on his way.

Surprisingly, I'm able to dedicate the next hour to searching for decorations, and just when I'm about to give up, I locate a janitor's closet near the morgue with two commercial-sized boxes labeled *Christmas*.

"Jackpot," I whisper to myself, tossing the top to one of the bins off to the side. It's a jumbled mess full of lights, garland, inflatables, and window clings, but I'm optimistic I can work with the forgotten treasures.

Looking around, I search for anything that might help me bring the bins upstairs—a hand truck, utility cart, *something*—but there's nothing. Sinking to my knees, I resort to sorting through the outdated decor right here in the closet, knowing I can only bring what I can carry.

The strands of lights are rolled nicely, so I loop as many as I can around my arm, wearing them like an oversized cuff that I push up by my shoulder. The brightly colored window clings lie flat against their plastic backings, shaped like ornaments and Christmas trees. There's a few boxes of inflatables—the giant Santa, a gingerbread man drinking hot cocoa, and a dinosaur wearing a Santa hat look like the best options to bring upstairs. There's no way this trio won't make the patients laugh a little. My gaze catches on a few wooden hanging signs as I scoop everything into my arms... I can always come back for more.

I wobble my way down the long corridor and wait as patiently as possible for the elevator. My plan of attack is to decorate the main halls of the children's wing, labor and delivery, and the ICU, then head back down for more.

I'll make as many trips as I need to if it means adding some extra happiness to the halls.

A rush of excitement trickles through me with every sparkling strand of tinsel I hang and every small detail I add to the halls of the hospital. The inflatables are inflated, and the garlands hung on pillars around the nurses' stations. Window clings have been placed, and I even went so far as to have a delivery service bring me paint markers to decorate the glass. Everything feels more cheerful already—like the Christmas magic is seeping into the bones of the building. The only thing left to do is to hang the lights, which should be easy, since the Chief gave me permission to hammer small nails near the ceiling to hang them.

It took a little convincing, but eventually I wore her down with promises to remove them within a week and to make sure to fix any noticeable holes. Virtually a nonexistent price to pay for the endorphin rush hearing the words *sure go ahead* invoked.

The morning's been filled with praise from my co-workers and words of encouragement from the loved ones of patients visiting. I've been spurred on by the smiles and filled with the Christmas spirit with every twinkling light shining from the strand of bulbs.

Now, as I balance on a rickety ladder leaned against the wall down in the ER, I work to hang the last of the lights. The San Diego sky is dark and dreary as I peek out the windows I'm balanced between, the snow still falling, covering the parking lot in a downy of white.

My head shakes on its own accord, still in complete disbelief that for the first time in *forever* we're having a white Christmas.

The *thud, thud, thud* of my hammer echoes through the halls as I secure the final nail before I spread my feet just a little wider on the rung of the metal I'm standing on, settling in a wider stance so I can unravel the lights.

"Christmas (Baby Please Come Home)" is stuck in my head, and I can't help but laugh in agreement that this Christmas is not like Christmas at all—stuck at the hospital, snow falling outside—but I'm riding the high of my decorating binge, and *nothing* can put a damper on my mood.

"What the hell are you doing up there, Genesis? You're going to fall!" Lincoln's alarmed baritone thunders from below me.

Startled, the strand of warm LEDs falls from my hand, swinging from where they hang limply over the one nail I managed to secure them on. Beneath my feet, the ladder wobbles.

"Jesus, Lincoln!" My hand slaps against the wall as though it'd be enough to hold me steady. "What the hell?"

He releases a low rumble, his fingers curling around the side of the ladder. "'What the hell' is right."

Swallowing thickly, I snap out of the stupor he's put me in, ignoring the relentless beat of my heart, and pick up the Christmas lights again. "What are you doing here, Doctor Stokes? You told me you were off today."

"Merry Christmas to you too, Nurse Nikolaou." There's sarcasm in his voice, and I sneak a glance down. The storm outside is nothing like the storm behind Lincoln's fire-filled stare, his normally bright blue eyes dimmed with anger.

I'm caught off guard—confused, and I immediately

feel vulnerable. Masking it with attitude, I ask, "What's your problem?"

"My problem is you're on a ladder older than both of our ages combined, leaning against the wall in a highly populated hallway where you could easily be knocked down."

A chill runs down my spine at the protectiveness in his tone, and I do everything I can to stifle the triumphant smile pulling at my lips. I loop a section of Christmas lights over another nail. "Careful, Lincoln. It almost sounds like you don't hate me."

"Of course I don't hate you," he snaps. I peek at him again, but this time he's watching the other nurses and doctors urgently power walk past us.

"Could have fooled me." My fingers graze the head of another nail as I loop a section around it, balancing on one foot as I reach for it. "What happened? Why are you here?"

Three more nails and I'm done. Climbing down the ladder, I hop from the third to last rung, landing practically chest to chest with Doctor Scrooge.

"In case you haven't noticed, it's snowing outside, and the ER is busier than a zoo."

I have to crane my neck to look at him as he towers over me. With my hands on my hips, I shrug. "I've been busy making this place a winter wonderland."

"I can see that."

"Doctor Stokes, Doctor Grimes is looking for you." A blonde nurse whizzes past us so quickly, I don't even catch who it is. When I turn back to face Lincoln, his gaze hasn't wavered. The butterflies in my stomach flutter in a frenzy.

Still staring at me, his eyes narrow just a beat. "No more ladders."

Then his phone vibrates in his pocket, pulling his attention. He starts to walk away before I can articulate a coherent thought, but somehow I manage to call out, "Merry Christmas to you too."

An exasperated sigh chuffs past my lips as I move the ladder down the wall to finish hanging the lights. Muttering under my breath, I climb the metal rungs again, annoyed.

Who the hell does he think he is, practically telling me I'm not capable of using a ladder?

I cast a glance in the direction Lincoln went, seeing him deep in conversation with another doctor and a couple nurses just a few yards away. Shaking my head with irritation, my hands and feet work in tandem to climb the next rungs, but the ladder wobbles unsteadily beneath me. My breath catches in my throat, heart seizing as I see the top of the ladder isn't flat against the wall, but teeters on the recessed edge of the wall.

Redistributing my balance, I root my feet, and the ladder stops quaking, unlike my pulse.

I'm okay. I can reach the next two nails and not worry about the third.

Reaching up, I hook the strand of lights over the nail, securing it in place before I switch hands to reach for the next, but it's enough to destabilize the ladder once again.

As the ladder sways, my sweaty palms slip from the metal, my feet flailing as I try to use my hands to catch myself. Everything happens so quickly, and a wave of nausea slams through me. My heart plummets when a scream pierces through the air.

Then I realize the scream is my own and I'm falling.

Chapter Eight

LINCOLN

I've been through many fear-inducing situations in my life, especially once I stepped into my profession.

As a child, I watched my cousin split his chin when the handlebars of his bike clipped a mailbox.

When I was in high school, I was house sitting for my best friend's family and lost their dog for almost a full twenty-four hours.

I've watched patients flatline on my operating table.

All scenarios sent me into a panic-stricken whirlwind which had me wondering if I was going into cardiac arrest.

"There's only two options for the poor bloke." Doctor Connors pores over a patient file for the millionth time, swiping his index finger in a forward motion to skim through the document on his tablet. "We operate, or he has no chance of survival."

The fluorescent lighting bounces off the screen, making it impossible for me to see the information he's looking at. But I don't need to see it to know exactly what he's talking about. We've been going around and around for the last three hours. "Which we've been over countless times, Connors. But as we've also discussed, it's a high-risk procedure. Survival is low regardless. At this point he's on borrowed time."

"What does the family say?" Doctor Lambert, a trauma surgeon, pushes his bifocals higher up the bridge of his nose.

Connors opens his mouth, but I cut him off. "They want what's best for their loved one. They want his doctors to see him as a person, and not just an opportunity to perform a rare surgery."

Doctor Connors huffs and drops the arm holding the tablet so it hangs limply by his side. His eyes narrow on me as though he believes he has any authority over me whatsoever. "It's a once in a lifeti—"

A high pitched scream penetrates the hall, cutting straight through the syllable Connors was speaking, and pierces straight through me.

Now I realize I've never known fear until *this* moment.

My head whips in the direction it came from, and I'm horrified as I watch Genesis's body hit the epoxied flooring. A sickening *crack* I can hear even from this far down the hall permeates the air and has bile rising in my throat.

Not a thought passes through my mind before I'm sprinting to her, my shoes squeaking as I practically leap the last few steps, slamming to my knees down on the floor in front of her.

"Genesis!" Brushing the hair from her face, her eyes are shut, and my heart sinks. "Gen, can you hear me?"

Soft bursts of air come from her nostrils, and I know she's still breathing, but even as I tap her shoulder, she doesn't rouse.

"Someone get me a response team, NOW! And a cervical collar, immediately!"

The fear coursing through me turns my blood to ice. How could this have happened? And on Christmas— her favorite damn holiday.

Still kneeling, I stare down at Gen, urging her to wake up. My voice is a whispered mutter as I beg her to open her eyes. I'm a goddamn doctor, yet my fingers are trembling against her warm, velvet skin. "Wake up, Gen, c'mon."

There's a sharp aching in my chest as I watch her lying unnaturally still on the floor.

"We'll take it from here, Doctor Stokes." The response team comes up behind me, wheeling a gurney.

Rising to my feet, I nod once and step back to give them space. My throat tightens.

This.

Watching the woman I've been desperately trying to deny and hide my feelings for, injured and practically lifeless, unknowing of how hard her head hit the floor, or what her condition may be. Knowing her favorite day of the year was just ruined because I was careless and walked away without spotting her on that rickety old ladder.

Not knowing when she'll wake up.

This is what real fear feels like.

Chapter Nine

GENESIS

The whirring buzz of machines is the first thing I hear when I wake up, followed by my pulse thumping in my eardrums.

It doesn't take a rocket scientist to realize I'm currently a patient in my own place of work, but I'm unsure if the muffled voices I hear are the product of a dream or not. The throbbing in my head is enough to keep my eyes and mouth closed, and I quickly tumble back into a dreamless slumber.

The next time I wake, the room is cloaked in darkness, and I'm even more discombobulated than before.

Is it still Christmas?

Placing my palms flat on the bed, I slide myself up, moving as gingerly as possible. An IV protrudes from the crook of my arm, the weight of it sitting sharp in my vein.

Finally, my eyes adjust, and I'm able to find the bed's remote and press the call button for a nurse, followed by the light.

It casts a dim glow above where I lay, and a gasp hitches in my throat when I see someone resting in the uncomfortable pleather chair beside me.

What is he doing here?

"Lincoln?" His name escapes me before I can stop myself, but it's not enough to rouse him.

Surely, I'm concussed and he's a figment of my imagination.

"Oh, good! You're awake. How are you feeling, dear?" Nurse Edwin's familiar smile comforts me as she walks into my room. There's a hospital cup in her hand she extends to me, already anticipating my request for water.

"Foggy." The cool drink slides down my throat, soothing the dryness.

"That's to be anticipated." Walking over to the machines, she jots down my vitals in my patient file on her tablet. "Can I get you anything?"

"Details," I croak, then curl my lips around the straw again. There's a strong possibility I might drink this entire cup.

"Your doctor—"

"No. You."

Nurse Edwin sighs, then glances at Lincoln.

"He's out," I assure her. "Please."

"You fell, dear. Hit your head pretty hard and initially were out for almost thirty minutes, which is worrisome, but aside from a concussion, your tests are all coming back normal. We've let you sleep the rest of the day to promote your healing. "

Concussion—I figured, but that explains the headache.

What it doesn't explain is why Mister Grinchy is asleep in the hideous, horribly uncomfortable armchair next to me.

I jut my thumb in his direction. "Why's he here?"

Nurse Edwin's lips purse with a hint of a smile. "He's been here the entire day. Refused to leave your side."

Refused to leave my—

"What?"

The look of confusion must have been evident on my face because Nurse Edwin laughs. "You heard me. Seems like Doctor Stokes is a little smitten with you, Genesis."

A chortle flies from my throat, which actually really hurts. Wincing, I shake my head. "More like hates me.

He's probably here to be the first to know if I keeled over."

"It's a thin line between love and hate."

"Not that thin." To distract myself from the craziness of this conversation, I take another drink of my water.

"I'll let the doctor know you're awake, Genesis. She should be in shortly."

Nurse Edwin is halfway through the door when I ask, "Who's my doctor?"

"Doctor Kelley."

Oh, good. I love Doctor Kelley. I've only gotten to work with her once, but she was lovely and very thorough.

Leather squeaks beside me and my attention shifts back to Lincoln. It appears he's only moved in his sleep, but something tells me he's coherent enough to hear me.

"What's the actual reason you're here, Lincoln? Did Zee tell you to watch over me?"

The room stays silent with the exception of the machines I'm hooked up to. Studying his face, I see the slight twitch of his eyes as they work to stay shuttered.

"C'mon, now. We both know you're awake. Answer my question."

Finally, the light blue shade of his irises connects with mine like magnets, and my heart bottoms out.

"How are you feeling, Gen?" he asks, voice thick with sleep.

"Woozy, and like my head might explode. You?"

"Sassy as always. Glad you're feeling better." Shoving the thin hospital blanket off his torso, he stands, coming to my side.

I crane my neck, searching his eyes. "Why are you here?"

Lincoln's lips part for a moment before he swallows thickly, his Adam's apple bobbing. I track the motion, making me mirror the nervous reflex. The air sizzles between us, feeling charged in a way I can't explain, but it's not unwelcome.

Stepping closer, he reaches out and pushes a strand of hair behind my ear, smoothing the tendril between his fingers until he reaches the end.

"It's a thin line between love and hate, Genesis."

Chapter Ten

LINCOLN

Gen's cheeks turn a deep shade of crimson at my words, shocked and flustered at my near admission. But where part of me feels like I've said too much, the other part wants to continue to admit my feelings for her.

As my fingers run to the end of her silky, curly hair, I let them fall back to my side, not allowing me to reach out and kiss her like I long to do. Instead I admire her for a moment, taking in every bit of her beauty—the ethereal glow of sun-kissed skin, the vibrancy of her sky-blue eyes.

There *is* a thin line between love and hate, but I've never once hated her. Not for a second. No one has ever captured my attention like she has, even if she's driving me crazy ninety-nine point nine percent of the time.

And pretending like I'm not completely infatuated with the woman in front of me is exhausting.

"I don't hate you, Gen. I could never hate you."

Her lips part. Questions swirl in the reflection of her eyes right before she squeezes them shut. "Why are you here, Lincoln?"

I stop denying the contact I've been craving, and I take her hand in mine. A small gasp catches in my throat, and it sends a spike of arousal through me. "You scared me. When I saw you hit the floor... Dammit, Gen."

Fear slithers down my spine as the image flashes through my memory.

Gen shakes her head. "I'm so confused."

"I'm not expecting anything. I only stayed because I wanted to make sure you were okay. I can leave." Slowly, I withdraw my hand from hers.

She surprises me when she catches it, tightening her grip. "No. Stay."

We're both held captive by the moment, eyes searching as our gazes stay locked. So many things are on the tip of my tongue, but I don't want to overwhelm her, not when she has a concussion, but I refuse to live in a lie any longer.

There's a million reasons why I should keep my distance like I have been, or why I should put a stop to this before it even begins, but between watching her fall, and witnessing her on a date not too long ago, I'm done.

I want *her*.

For the first time in a long time, I feel nervous to speak to a woman. "Gen, I—"

"There she is!" Doctor Kelley glides into the room, breaking the tension in the air and interrupting what I was about to say. "It's so good to see you awake, Nurse Nikolaou. How are you feeling?"

With my hypothetical tail tucked between my legs, I back away from Genesis. As her hand falls from mine and hits the side of her hospital bed, she looks at me in disarray rather than greeting her doctor.

I try to reassure her with a smile. "I'll give you a minute. I'm going to give Miller and Zee an update."

"My family!" she gasps.

"Are waiting for their update as well."

Doctor Kelley buzzes around the monitors, inputting updates into her tablet. My eyes wander to her, knowing she's purposely making herself productive right now, then back to Gen.

"You spoke to my parents?" She pushes herself more upright, then starts patting the space around her while frantically looking around. "Where's my phone? I have to call them."

"Your mother." I turn around and grab her phone off

the windowsill, where it was charging, and hand it to her. "I'll call them too. Let Doctor Kelley go over things with you. I'll be back."

Slipping out into the hallway, I call my cousin as I lean against the wall, pinching the bridge of my nose.

"I screwed up," I groan the moment he answers.

Ignoring my juvenile call for attention, he asks, "How's Genesis?"

"Awake. Stable. Slightly less annoying than usual and therein lies the problem, Miller."

"What are you talking about?"

"*Genesis!*" Her name falls from my lips in a hiss of frustration. "I may have crossed a line with her."

Miller doesn't bother hiding his exasperation. "What kind of line?"

"Who is it?" Zee's groggy voice comes through the phone, accompanied by a hearty yawn.

"It's Linc." Miller mirrors her yawn, and his breath obnoxiously blows into the receiver.

"Did I wake you guys? It's only"—I glance at my watch—"eight thirty."

"How's Gen?" Zee asks with concern at the same moment Miller clarifies, "You're on speaker, and no, but we were watching a movie."

Talking over Miller again, Zee rapid fires questions

at me. "Has she woken up? Can I talk to her? When can she go home?"

"Take a breath, Zee. She's alright. Awake, sipping on water, nursing her headache."

She sighs in relief. "Thank goodness. A Christmas miracle."

I wouldn't call it that, but sure, a Christmas miracle it is.

"I've been so worried all day and have felt *super* guilty for enjoying my Christmas while my friend's in the hospital. Have you called her parents yet?"

"Not yet. Honestly, it should be Gen's doctor who calls them, but I will after we hang up. But first I need to speak with Miller."

"I'm here." Static filters through from the phone being passed off.

"As I was saying, I screwed up." Walking down the hall of the hospital, I step into a quiet alcove and lean against the wall.

"How so," Miller grumbles. There's a faint sound of bedding being shuffled, then footsteps. "You're not on speaker anymore. I'm in the other room."

"Appreciate the discretion, although it's not really needed. I'm sure Zee will hear about it soon."

"So what'd you do?"

"I came onto her."

A nurse passes by, catching my eye. She gives me a

small wave, and I nod politely before shifting my body, closing off any chance of conversation.

"What do you mean you came onto her? I didn't even know you had a thing for her."

I exhale slowly. "Well, I guess I've done a damn good job at concealing it then." Bitterness fuels me, and I rub my hand over my jaw in frustration.

"Seriously?" Miller asks, still in disbelief. "How long have you had feelings for her, man?"

I pinch the bridge of my nose. "Since the day Zee introduced us."

"Why haven't you said anything?" I can practically see my cousin mouth *what the fuck* to himself as he paces.

"What is there to say?" Leaning my head back against the wall, I close my eyes briefly. "You *finally* found someone who makes you happy. I'm not going to jeopardize your relationship by dating her friend."

A long silence settled between us, and with it, I could hear the crackling of the fireplace on the other end of the phone. I was right, he's still at my parents' house.

I should end the call and let him get back to his Christmas.

"How would you dating Genesis put *my* relationship in jeopardy?"

"You know damn well that if I'd gone for Gen and it didn't work out, things would always be weird between me and Zee. We could never hang as a friend group like we do now. You're telling me that wouldn't strain your relationship?"

Another silence sat heavy between us, and I let him process what I'd said.

Part of the reason why I haven't pursued her is to protect his relationship, in some capacity. In hindsight, as we talk this out, I realize I never should have. He didn't ask me to, and he wouldn't have.

I did this to myself.

"I mean, when you put it that way, yeah, I guess, but we're also *adults*. If you have a genuine interest in Genesis, your concern doesn't seem like enough of a reason to not go for her. I mean, look at how Zee and I got together. She was your date for Christmas last year."

"My *fake* date," I reminded him, letting out a low laugh.

"Still, you brought her around, and I stole her from you."

"Yeah, you kind of did, didn't you?" Glancing at my watch again, I wonder if Doctor Kelley has finished with Gen yet. I'm anxious to go back in there. Speaking to her is far more important than this conversation.

"Anyway, what happened with Genesis?"

"I threw all caution to the wind." Pushing my hand through my hair, I stop walking, looking around the quiet hallway. "It's like something snapped inside of me when I watched her fall."

Miller lets out a low, taunting whistle. "Then go get your girl, Lincoln. I thought you said she was awake."

"She is." Like a magnet, my gaze drifts down the hallway toward her room. The door's still closed. "She's with her doctor now, but they should be finishing up."

"What the hell are you still doing on the phone with me?" The smile on his face was evident in his tone. It's contagious, and with a nod of my head he can't see, I move in her direction.

"We'll talk later, Miller."

Ending the call, I practically sprint, my steps quickening as I head for Gen. Reaching for the doorknob, I'm surprised when it opens from inside, and I'm suddenly face to face with Doctor Kelley.

"Oh, Doctor Stokes, there you are." She steps further into the hall, closing the door behind her.

"How is she?" I peer over Doctor Kelley's shoulder through the small window on the door, but the light in the room is dim, making it difficult to see.

"She's doing as expected. Headache and fatigue, with some light sensitivity. I'd discharge her tonight, but in my opinion, better safe than sorry."

"I completely agree." Nodding, I try to look around her again. I'm anxious—dare I say desperate to get in there.

My phone buzzes against my leg, the vibration jarring, and it pulls me back to reality.

"Lincoln, are you okay?" Doctor Kelley's voice muddles the haze in my mind, but her words don't process enough for me to answer her.

My stomach tightens when I see the number I called earlier flash across my screen. Gen's mom.

"So sorry, Doctor, I need to take this." Smashing my thumb against the accept button, I press the device against my ear. "Hello?"

"Hi, Doctor Stokes?"

"Mrs. Nikolaou, hi."

"Hi, dear. I hope I'm not bothering you, but Peter and I were getting ready to head down to the hospital. Is now a good time?" Her voice trembles, the worry clutching her tightly.

"I'm sure she'd love that, Mrs. Nikolaou. Her doctor just left the room and gave me an update." I regurgitate everything Doctor Kelley just told me, giving her factual information in my standard monotone voice I reserve for this exact scenario. As I'm relaying everything though, I glance out the window across from me, seeing the snowstorm. I've never seen anything like it before, not here in the city at least. "Mrs. Nikolaou, can I order you a car so you're not driving in this weather?"

"You're so kind, but we'll make do. It's about time we put the truck to good use. We'll be there in about thirty minutes or so."

With a promise to update them if anything changes, I slip my phone back in my pocket. Pausing outside of her door, I blow out a shaky breath. Miller told me to go get my girl, but what if she's not interested in being *mine*?

The thought forms a lump in my throat as my fingers graze the handle of the door.

I'll never know until I tell her how I feel. How I've *been* feeling.

Pushing the door open, I step into Gen's room. It takes a second for my eyes to adjust to the pale, dim lighting, and once they do, I find she's already drifted off to sleep again.

For a moment I watch the steady rise and fall of her chest, letting it ease the tightness in my chest.

She's so beautiful.

So mine.

At least, I hope she'll be.

Chapter Eleven

GENESIS

"Mom, stop. I'm okay." I swat away her hand as she tries to fluff my pillow for the sixth time. I'm propped in my bed with more pillows surrounding me than I could ever need, two bottles of water, snacks, three paperbacks I haven't started, and my TV remote. It's slightly overwhelming.

From my side, Pebbles yawns, overly dramatic and loud.

"I know you're okay, Gennie. I just want to make sure you're comfortable while you're left here all alone. You gave us quite a scare."

"It's just a mild concussion, Mom. I promise I'll survive it. In fact, I'll be back up and functioning within the next couple of hours, if you would just stop fussing over me and let me take a nap!" To appease her, I take a swig of water from one of the bottles.

"Never! I'm your mother. I'll fuss over you until the day I die." She pulls the blanket further up my chest.

Glancing at my phone, a new message from Lincoln pops up, sending a rush of excitement through me. He's fussing over me just as much as my mother is, although his level of concern is a bit more shocking, considering the disinterest he's shown since...well, since we met.

"Is that handsome doctor checking on you again?" my mom asks inquisitively, pushing her hands underneath my sides to tuck the blanket.

The warmth of a blush stains my cheeks. "Yeah. I'm sure he just wants to know how my headache is."

Throbbing, but not as much as the place between my thighs whenever I think about the tension between us when he tucked my hair behind my ear yesterday.

Swiping my thumb across the screen, I peek at his message.

Can I bring you dinner tonight? We should talk.

"So listen," my mom interrupts my internal monologue reading his message for the third time. "Since you're not in any condition to be driving today, your father and I thought we could bring the Christmas cele-bration to you. Would you be up for that?"

Dropping my phone into my lap, I return my attention back to her. When she leaves, I'll respond to him. "My kitchen is far too tiny for you to be cooking a full spread in, Mom."

"Nonsense. All I need is a counter, a stovetop, and an oven, and I can make do."

I can't avoid matching her smile. "It'll be tight, but I'd love nothing more."

Peeking down at my phone again, I glance at Lincoln's message. *Can I bring you dinner tonight?*

For a split second, my mind and my heart are at war. "Yeah, Mom. Let's have it here."

Leaning down, she presses a kiss against my fore-head. "Yay! I was hoping you'd say that. Get some rest, and we will be back in a few hours. Do I need to do anything for Pebbles before I leave?"

"Would you mind putting two scoops of food in her bowl? Her breakfast is already later than normal, and I'm surprised she's not gnawing at my hands like a starving beast." With a giggle, I roll my eyes and ruffle the fur between her ears.

"Of course I'll feed my granddog!" Mom's eyes roam over the nightstand and my bed, taking silent inventory of everything she's brought to me, ensuring I won't have to get up while she's gone.

"Go." I shoo my hands in her direction. "I'll be fine! I promise it's just a concussion, and I'm feeling better already."

"Okay. I love you." Her fingers tighten around mine affectionately.

"Love you too, Mom."

A few minutes later, the click of my front door lets me know she's gone. Sinking against my pillow, my eyes fall shut as the whirlwind of the last two days replays through my mind.

An exhausted laugh of disbelief slips past my lips. *I can't believe I fell off a ladder and gave myself a concussion on Christmas.*

And in an unexpected turn of events, Lincoln... has *feelings* for me?

Speaking of which, I need to respond to him.

> I can't tonight.

> My family is coming over to celebrate Christmas.

> Tomorrow then.

> Tomorrow is the holiday party.

> You can't possibly tell me you're still planning on going to that.

Of course I am.

You have a concussion.

I know. People don't need to keep reminding me! I'm fine.

Do you need anything?

No, but thank you.

I watch the typing dots in our text thread appear and then disappear. It happens a couple of times before finally they vanish for good.

I'm not sure what to make of it, and for a moment I consider calling Zee, but I know I should rest before my family arrives later.

Plugging my phone into the charger next to me, I cuddle into my blankets. Despite the sunlight streaming in through the crack in my curtains, I'm off to dreamland in no time, dancing with the sugarplum fairies.

"Everything smells delicious," I compliment my mom as I shuffle into the kitchen, clad in fuzzy socks, an oversized Christmas sweater, and my pajama bottoms.

Nothing I'm wearing matches, but being that it's just my family here, there's no pressure to change.

"You look like shit," my youngest brother comments with a smirk as I slide onto the barstool next to him.

His comment earns him a punch to the shoulder. "Well, I have an excuse, but I'm not sure what yours is."

We both laugh, and our mom shakes her head with a smile as she stirs something on my stove.

"We thought we'd keep it easy tonight. I hope that's okay."

"Of course. What's for dinner?"

"Turkey with savory stuffing, roasted lemon potatoes, spanakopita, salad, and melomakarona for dessert."

A hearty sense of nostalgia hits me. "Mom! I thought you weren't going to make a whole holiday spread?"

"You know your father enjoys his favorite Greek recipes for Christmas." She lifts her shoulders, grinning. "I couldn't resist."

Spinning on my barstool, I turn toward my father, who's lounging on my sofa watching highlights from a football game. "Where's everyone else?"

"I'm sure they'll be here soon. We didn't want to overwhelm you, so I told them to arrive later, just before dinner. How are you feeling?"

My eyes flick toward my brother, who's glued to his

phone. "So much better. My headache is completely gone now."

"That's wonderful, Gennie," Mom coos. "Just don't do too much. Let us take care of you."

For once, I don't argue with her. We fall into a comfortable silence, listening to the sportscaster talk football. It's exactly what I need in this moment, and I'm happy to have my parents and one of my brothers here.

Sometimes all a girl needs is her mama, and mine is nothing short of amazing.

The delicious scent of garlic and onions wafts into the air, and I turn back to watch my mother cook.

This is peaceful—I'm *happy*.

And even though things certainly didn't go as planned this Christmas, I can't help but feel content with the way the evening is turning out.

Then I remember—

"Did anyone bring the plastic wrap ball? Are we going to play?"

"Are you sure that's a good idea?" My brother gives me a condescending side-eye, finally removing his retinas from his phone and joining us back on planet Earth.

"Why wouldn't it be?"

"I don't know. I'm not the one with the concussion."

Everyone needs to stop focusing on me having a concus-

sion. It's really not that big of a deal. "You guys are acting like I lost a limb. I'm fine."

"If you insist," my mother murmurs, pulling open the oven and prodding the flakey, golden brown spanakopita with a wooden spoon. "Perfect, perfect."

The shrill sound of the doorbell ringing snaps my attention toward my entryway as my sister and my eldest brother burst through the door without waiting to be let in. Why they bothered ringing the doorbell is beyond me. They're bickering, voices competing in a familiar sibling banter they never outgrew.

Two hours later, my entire family is seated cross-legged around my coffee table, laughter filling the room. With full stomachs and smiles wide, we settle into playing the game we've all been anxiously waiting for. My dad's already geared up in a pair of pink oven mitts with strawberries on them, my mother waiting with red translucent dice in hand.

My heart is full, yet there's been a lingering thought in my mind that's been impossible to shake. With every glance I sneak at my phone, I circle back to the conversation I know I need to have with the one person who won't leave my thoughts.

Chapter Twelve

GENESIS

A light bout of dizziness hits as I stand in front of my bathroom mirror, applying makeup to my freshly washed face. I steady myself with a deep exhale, gripping the sides of the sink for balance. Preparing for my work's holiday party has been a whole process as I take things slow so I don't bring on another head rush.

After dinner and our game last night, my sister waited patiently as I took the world's longest shower. Then she gave me a blowout, smoothing my wild curls to silky perfection, which I ended up curling with my curling iron for a different look than usual.

My evening starts in fifteen minutes, but I have no problem being fashionably late. Showing up right on time would only make it more obvious I'm showing up alone.

As I swipe the mascara wand against my eyelashes, the glow of my phone catches my eye in the bathroom mirror. Pausing, wand suspended midair, I glance at the screen.

Lincoln called once this morning and texted me earlier this afternoon, both of which I ignored. He wants to talk, and I know it's a good idea if we do, but I'm also afraid.

My gut tells me his behavior while I was in the hospital was just a moment of vulnerability. A lapse of judgment. He's probably calling to apologize for flirting, and reaffirm he doesn't have feelings for me—romantically, or otherwise.

Frankly, I don't think my heart can take it.

Expelling a shaky breath, I return to the task at hand —applying my makeup and making myself look absolutely phenomenal for this Christmas party.

There's not a single soul I am interested in impressing other than myself, and after spending time wearing a hospital gown this week, I figure I owe it to myself to get a little dolled up.

Once my makeup is perfected, I strip down to my lacy thong and strapless bra, then grab my dress from where it hangs on the back of the bathroom door.

Layers of chocolate-brown tulle hang in an elegant skirt from a princess cut bodice, stealing my breath away for the hundredth time. I'm utterly obsessed with the uniqueness of the dress—such a simple design, in a neutral color, yet I've never seen anything more beautiful. Although it doesn't *scream* holiday party, the feeling I have when it's on my body is unmatched.

Sliding the dress on, I maneuver it into place, studying my reflection as the whole look comes together. When I'm satisfied, I turn the bathroom light off and return to my room.

As per usual, Pebbles stretches lazily on my bed, my presence pulling her from another slumber. She takes up more than half of the space on my duvet and seems to be in no hurry to move.

"I'll be back in a few hours, girl," I tell her as she yawns. "You stay out of trouble while I'm gone."

I assume she understood every word because her head plops back onto the mattress before my sentence has even finished.

The click of my heels echoes through my small apartment as I finish shutting off lights and closing the open doors to spaces Pebbles doesn't need access to. Then, I lock up, ready to meet my rideshare waiting for me downstairs.

Bright lights reflect off the tall buildings that make up San Diego's downtown, making them appear as though they are twinkling against the night sky. My driver takes me down North Harbor Drive, where I people and boat watch as we pass the bay.

When we pull up to the hotel, I thank the kind man for the ride. The lobby is bustling with activity as I quietly weave through, quickly spotting the elevators. I'm alone as I ride to the top floor.

I'm not sure what I expected this party to be like, but it certainly wasn't *this*. My jaw drops when the elevator doors slide open, revealing a decadent ballroom overlooking all of San Diego's downtown. Everywhere I look is draped in shades of silver. It covers the window treatments, the tables, even the centerpieces. The soft, low lighting shimmers against it, giving the space a glamorous ambiance. Deep burgundy accents are scattered throughout, adding a holiday richness.

My coworkers are dressed to the nines in gorgeous dresses and smart suits—a stark contrast to the scrubs and doctor's coats they're typically in.

Upbeat music blends with laughter and conversation, and for a moment, I take it all in.

The atmosphere instantly lifts my spirit, and as I step further inside the room, I'm overtaken with a sense of renewed energy. This is exactly what I've needed after the last couple of days, and I'm so glad I made the decision to come tonight.

"Genesis." Lincoln's low baritone freezes me, wrapping around me like a seductive embrace. A shiver shoots through my body, but it's met with a rush of heat low in my belly that ignites at the sound of my name on his lips.

Turning slowly, I see him take his final few steps before reaching me, hands in the pockets of his dark gray slacks. He's coupled it with a matching gray button-down, with the sleeves rolled up mid-forearm, and a dark, paisley pattern tie. It's hard to tell what color it is in this lighting, but he looks good.

Really good.

"I thought you weren't coming." My voice sounds far raspier than it should, and I sink my teeth into my bottom lip to keep myself from saying something stupid.

"We need to talk, and you're avoiding me."

"How can I be avoiding you when I haven't seen you?" The jest comes out naturally, but this time, a hint of regret follows.

The look on Lincoln's face is stoic. "I've sent you two text messages and called you, to which you have not acknowledged any of my attempts." He takes a step closer and picks up one of my curls, playing with it. "This is different," he murmurs.

My breathing hitches. "Bad different, or good different?"

"Just...different. You always look beautiful, Genesis."

My heart does a traitorous flip-flop, and the air around us suddenly thickens until it's hard to breathe. Part of me wants to walk away—to not hear him out—because the impending sting of rejection clings to me.

But the other part, the curious part, hangs on his every word, eager to listen. "What did you want to talk about?"

Lincoln glances around, gaze skimming over the ballroom full of our co-workers. "Can we go somewhere private?"

Every fiber of my being screams that this is a bad idea, but something has shifted between us. I can *feel* it. The idea of being alone with him is both exhilarating and terrifying. Still, I find myself nodding.

When he offers me the crook of his arm, I take it without hesitation, letting him guide me through the throng of people around us.

Back inside the elevator, he presses the button for the rooftop, taking us up another level.

Cold December air wraps around me as the door slides open. The rooftop is quiet—we're the only ones up here. The warmth of the heaters radiates, scattered between the abundance of seating, yet we move in silence until we reach the edge of the building.

Leaning against the railing, Lincoln's forearms rest

on the metal as he looks out toward the Coronado Bridge.

"I know I crossed the line with you while you were in the hospital," he says quietly, not looking in my direction. "As a doctor, I apologize for my inappropriate behavior."

"Lincoln, it's fi—" My response slips out immediately, but he cuts me off.

"But as a man, I won't apologize for showing you the fear I had seeing you get hurt. I'm not sorry for that, Gen. And if I'm being honest, I'm tired of pretending my feelings for you don't exist."

For the first time in my life, I'm speechless. Shadows from the night fall over his face, but I still see the glitter in his eye and the bashful smile upturning his lips.

"Are you serious?" I breathe, my heart pounding in disbelief. My nails dig into my palms as I try to steady myself.

The weight of the confession is woven through his words as he promises, "I would never lie to you."

I take a second, letting his words sink in. My mind's racing to catch up as this all feels akin to whiplash. For so long, he's made me believe he hates me, and now...

Now... My eyes squeeze together tightly, staying closed as I whisper, "All this time you've acted like I was the bane of your existence—like you absolutely could not stand me."

Tears threaten to spill through my lashes. I flinch when Lincoln's palm touches my cheek, turning my face in his direction. Hesitantly, I open my eyes.

"Completely enamored is more accurate," he confesses softly. "For the sake of my cousin and his newly developing relationship, I chose to mask my attraction for you with indifference. A poor choice on my part, but one I thought I was making in the best interest of Miller. I couldn't live with myself if I pursued something with his girlfriend's best friend and it didn't work out. I didn't want to be responsible for potentially ruining what *they* had."

"So why now? If you've been hiding it all this time, why change your mind now?" The words tumble from my lips, unable to hide the frustration laced within them. I've spent *months* trying to be his friend, knowing that would be the best-case scenario.

"Because I realized life is too short."

With a disbelieving huff, I shake my head. "You're a doctor, that's a no-brainer."

Running his hand through his hair, Lincoln's jaw tightens before he exhales through his nose. His eyes lock with mine, and he takes a step closer to me, even though we're practically chest to chest already.

"Let me be more specific then." Every word is slow, determined. "Watching you fall from that ladder terrified me more than any surgery I've ever performed—more than watching any patient fight for their life. It shook me to my core, and in that moment, everything I've been trying to bury into the recesses of my mind came crashing full force into the forefront. Even if you don't reciprocate my feelings, Genesis, I realized I'd rather tell you and face rejection then continue pretending I'm not enamored by every move you make."

Turning back toward the railing, I look out at the skyline. My hands tremble, and I wrap my fingers around the cold metal to keep it from being noticeable. So many things race through my mind, it's hard to process what he's saying. I want his words to be true, but after so long believing otherwise, I find it hard to trust so blindly.

"You're saying a lot of lovely words, Lincoln, but that's all they are—words. How can I be sure what you're saying is real?" A heavy ache sits in my chest, and as I turn back to Lincoln, I watch his lips part, ready to tell me otherwise, but the frustration inside of me pushes me to continue. "You know what? Fuck it, I'm just going to say it. I've had feelings for you for far longer than I care to admit. And if you're just playing with my emotions—"

"I'm not," he rushes to say, but I cut him off.

"Then *prove* it. *Show* me. We're both adults, and we've apparently been playing childish games for too long." A manic laugh bubbles from my lips as I toss my hands into the air, turning back to face him. "And for no reason it seems like. *So show me*, Lincoln. You want me? Take me then. I could have been yours this whole time."

Something darkens in his eyes, and his hand comes up to cradle my face again. His fingers slide along my jaw, gripping me possessively as he holds me in place. Heat surges through me, pooling low in my belly. "You want me to show you, Genesis?" Our eyes remain locked, and for the first time, I see another side to Doctor Lincoln Stokes—a side I'm eager to explore. Leaning into me, his breath dusts the shell of my ear as he growls, "Prove to you what I'm feeling is legitimate?"

A wolfish smile spreads across his face as he draws back slowly, a silent challenge burning in his eyes.

I feel like I could morph into a puddle at his feet from the heat in his piercing stare. Raising my chin, I don't dare blink. "Yes."

No sooner does the word leave my mouth are his lips crashing against mine. His tongue gains access without hesitation, and there's nothing gentle about it. No softness or restraint, only raw, consuming *need*.

Months of pent-up longing pours out between us, tasting sweet and electric.

Growling into my mouth, Lincoln closes what minuscule distance there was between us, molding his body against mine as he cages me against the railing. My back arches as the evidence of his arousal drives against me, strong and hard.

A breathy sigh escapes me. *I can't believe this is happening.*

"Do you want more proof, Gen?" He groans against my mouth.

My arms encircle his neck, pulling him closer. "Yes."

He kisses me again, and I melt into him, getting lost in the moment. We're both out of breath when he finally breaks the trance, pulling away with a mischievous glint in his eye. "Will the validity of my words mean more to you if I show you from my knees?" Slowly, he breaks from my hold, sinking down, letting his hand glide against the side of my body until he's low enough to shift it to the inside of my thigh.

My legs tremble as I look down at him through hooded eyes, watching as his hand wraps around my ankle before he trails it back up my leg.

"Lincoln." His name slips off my tongue, floating on the wind.

Curling his fingers around the tulle, he lifts my dress, exposing more of my legs. He presses higher onto his knees, kissing the tops of my thighs.

"Part of the reason I put a wall between us is because I thought I didn't deserve a woman like you. So sweet." *Another kiss.* "So sunshine-y." *And another.*

Sliding my fingers into his hair, I tilt his head back, forcing him to meet my gaze. With narrowed eyes, and a smile tugging at my lips, I murmur, "You're an idiot."

His fingers tighten against my skin. "I know."

"So long as you acknowledge it. Keep going." Releasing his hair, my hand drifts to the top of his shoulder.

Taking it as an invitation, he reaches down and grabs my ankle, guiding my leg to rest over his other shoulder. My eyes widen as I realize what he's doing as he hikes my dress up more, exposing my black lace thong, and the cool air hits my center. "Lincoln—" I warn, but he shakes his head, kissing the skin just below the apex of my thighs.

My knees buckle when his nose rubs against my clit, the stimulation even more intense because of the rough lace acting as a barrier. I cry out, my head tilting back as I look into the inky night sky.

Pulling away the fabric, Lincoln swipes his tongue

up my slit before his lips suction around the most sensitive part of me. I cry out, my hand flying back to his hair to steady myself as he brings his fingertips to my center.

"You're dripping for me, Gen," he muses as he laps up my wetness. "How is it that you even manage to taste like Christmas, too?"

Pressing one finger into me, my grip tightens on his hair to keep myself from falling as unintelligible moans cascade from my lips.

"Sugar, spice, and *happiness*. I've never tasted anything so delicious."

Swirling the tip of his tongue around my clit, he presses another finger into me, letting the two pump in a steady rhythm. My arousal slides down my thigh as he torturously thrusts into me again and again.

"You're glistening." His tongue glides against my inner thigh, not letting a drop of it go to waste. "God, Gen. I'll spend forever proving myself to you if this is my reward."

I open my mouth to speak, but no words come out, my mind completely useless as pleasure overtakes every sense and thought I have. There's only one word repeating through my mind like a mantra.

More.

"I need more," I whimper, my fingers clawing at Lincoln's shirt in a desperate attempt to get him to stand.

Groaning, he sucks my clit harder, and tugs before he rises. But I hardly have a chance to catch my breath before he grabs my chin, tilting my head firmly to connect us again. Stealing the air from my lungs, he claims me through his kiss.

Pinning me with his body, he kneads my breast as my hands explore him, taking in each ripple of muscle beneath his dress shirt, every ridge of his abdomen.

Another low rumble erupts from him, and he breaks the kiss, spinning me around. I choke on a gasp, suddenly facing the twinkling lights of the city. Lincoln's touch is gentle yet unyielding as he pushes me into the railing, my stomach firm against it as my hands wrap around the metal on their own accord.

Pulling my thong down, he leaves it just above my knees before pressing his hand against my center again, playing with my folds and opening them wide as he strokes me with his fingers.

"*Fuck*, Gen." His forehead rests against my shoulder. "This wasn't what I was expecting by coming here tonight. I want to *prove* to you how much I want you—over and over again if you'll let me—but I didn't bring protection."

Is it wrong of me to not give a shit?

My knees buckle as he fucks me slowly with his hand,

curving the two fingers pressed inside of me so he can stroke my G-spot. His motions are slow—deliberate. A much different pace than the frenzy from two minutes ago.

I need him. Now. I don't care if it's wrong, or reckless. I just want *him*.

Reaching behind me, I unbuckle his belt with one hand, maneuvering my hand to unhook his button and lower his zipper before I reach inside, taking his length in my hand. Slowly, I stroke the velvety skin of his shaft, mirroring the pace of his fingers inside me.

There's a subconscious part of me that knows anyone could walk onto this roof right now and catch us, and for some reason, that makes it all the more exhilarating.

Turning my head toward Lincoln's, I catch his lips. His cock twitches in my hand, and I can't stand the emptiness I feel even with his fingers inside of me. I crave all of him. "*Please*, Lincoln."

"Are you sure?" His voice is so gravely, my knees weaken again.

"*Prove it,*" I whisper, repeating my sentiment from earlier.

Prove it.

Take me.

His belt clinks as he pushes his pants down slightly,

trading my hand for his own as he aligns himself. Soft lips press against my shoulder, peppering kisses in a trail that leads to my neck as he presses into me with one swift thrust.

My gasp melds with his low groan, and he gives me a moment to adjust to the size of him. He feels incredible, like he was meant to fit inside of me. I clench around him, pushing back to take him deeper.

"Move," I beg breathlessly. His hand slides to splay against my stomach, and I lay mine against it, lacing our fingers together.

Lincoln follows my instruction, pulling out almost completely before he presses into me again. As his long, fluid thrusts fill me, the sound of our skin slapping against each other catches in the breeze. We don't speak, but our moans tell a story of their own.

Sliding his hand further down my body, his fingers find my clit again as he rolls his hips into me relentlessly. My eyes roll back before I squeeze them shut—the world tilting on its axis as my body inches closer and closer to release.

"Gen, I—you're—" Lincoln fumbles over his words, his fingers working me harder. "I'm close."

Words fail me as I tumble over the edge, free falling into my orgasm before I can even tell him I'm close too.

My body spasms against his, my core clenching around his shaft tightly, euphoric from how it feels inside me as I come.

"Fuck," he slurs, his forearms slamming against the railing as he chases his own release, thrusting into me with a rough possessiveness. "You're fucking drenching me, Gen. So. Fucking. Wet. And. Hot."

A low, primal rumble tears from him as he stills, his forehead dropping between my shoulder blades while he catches his breath.

With a shaky laugh, I grab his hand and tangle his fingers with mine. For a moment, we're both still, coming down from the high, until a shiver runs through me, the cold night air licking against the sheen of sweat gathered across the back of my neck.

Slowly—*torturously*—he withdraws from me, and I clench around air at the loss of him.

He takes a step back, and I adjust my panties and my dress.

With a nervous laugh, I turn to face him. "Well, I'd call that proving it."

Quirking a brow, he fixes his belt buckle. "You think I'm done?"

Lincoln takes a step closer, and instinctively, I take one back. Catching my wrist, he brings my palm to his lips and presses a kiss against it.

"Aren't you?"

His hand glides down the length of my arm before lacing our fingers together, giving me a gentle tug, guiding me back to—I assume—the party. "Not even close, Gen. I've got all night." Then, with a playful grin, he adds, "Let's get out of here."

Chapter Thirteen

GENESIS

I'm riding cloud nine, still wrapped in Lincoln's arms after spending the night in his bed. My hand rests on his chest as it rises and falls, the slow beat of his heart beneath my palm. He's warm against me, keeping me cozy in his cool apartment. Lazily, he traces circles against my arm with his fingertip, occasionally pressing soft kisses against my skin.

With every touch, I find myself melting further into him, wondering how I couldn't see straight through him before.

The central heat clicks on, filling the room with a burst of warmth. I snuggle deeper, my body molding perfectly with his. Last night felt like a dream, and I'm still completely awestruck by the turn of events.

"What do you want to do today?" Lincoln's voice is

rough with sleep. Turning onto his side, he faces me, hair tousled, eyes still heavy.

The butterflies in my stomach stir—he's devastatingly handsome.

A smile purses my lips. "Are you asking me to spend the day with you?"

"I don't plan on letting you go, if that's the question," he volleys easily.

Not only was that not the question, but his answer has me swallowing thickly, willing myself to not roll over onto him and get round four started...or would it be five?

It's too soon to be feeling what I am—it could still be fleeting.

A holiday fling.

But God, I hope not.

"What did you have in mind?" I ask as cooly as I can muster.

"Well, I know your Christmas wasn't exactly what you had expected. Would you like to go see the lights at the botanical garden this evening? I can buy us tickets."

Excitement flares through me brightly, like a strand of lights being plugged in. "I've never been! I've heard it's beautiful."

Beaming, I sit up, turning to face him. The sheet

slips from my chest, exposing me, and Lincoln's eyes drift down.

Snapping his gaze back to mine, he nods decidedly. "Then let's go."

"Really? You hate Christmas!"

He shrugs, a small smile tugging at his lips as he sits up next to me. "It's not Christmas anymore," he points out, then kisses me.

"You know what I mean."

Lincoln grins—actually *fully* grins, and it's beautiful. "I do. And yes, Gen, really. I don't hate Christmas, I just don't love it like you do."

"Well, that's because you've never experienced the holiday with me." I clap my hands together. "Get dressed, Stokes. We're celebrating my favorite holiday."

I have no idea what adventure we're about to embark on, but I'm good at thinking quick on my feet. My instinct is to take him ice skating, but I know I can do better than that. Ice skating is the obvious choice—I want today to be special.

Lincoln swings his legs over the edge of the bed, tugging at my hand playfully, trying to pull me with him. Swatting him away, I tell him to go, and grab my phone off his nightstand as he disappears into his en suite.

"How long does it take you to shower?" I call after him as the water turns on, scrolling through my apps.

"Fifteen, maybe twenty minutes," he yells back, and a few seconds later I hear the shower door close.

Perfect. Just enough time to plan the ultimate San Diego *belated* Christmas. Pulling his comforter over my body, I snuggle back into the warmth of his bed and get to work.

An hour later we're exiting the cutest bakery in Logan Heights, a box of freshly made conchas in hand as we head back to Lincoln's SUV. A dollar store bag sits in the backseat, filled with discounted costume accessories such as Santa hats, holiday-themed light-up necklaces, and glasses shaped like reindeer heads.

Also in the back is a fluffy red blanket for us to lay out on the beach, which is where we're heading now.

"Are you sure you want to go to Mission Bay?" Lincoln asks, glancing at me from the driver's seat.

He's doing those effortlessly sexy things guys do where they steer with their wrists and make smooth turns with the palms of their hands. I can't explain why I like that as much as I do, but it's making me want to ask him to pull the car over.

Nodding vigorously, I narrow my eyes. "Sorry to break it to you, but you're not getting out of breakfast on the beach."

By the time our toes hit the sand, there's not a cloud in the sky, and the bright shade of blue reflects off the navy water. White foam lines the shore, leaving broken remnants of shells as waves roll against the sand, then recede back into the ocean.

Lincoln spreads the blanket on the warm, dry sand, giving it a light shake so it stretches wide enough for both of us. As usual, the beach is busy, but today there's an easy, laid-back energy as families relax post-Christmas.

Sitting, I crack open the bakery box we brought and reveal the delicious assortment of concha bread, reaching for a pink one. It's soft and pliable between my fingers, and my mouth waters as I take my first bite. The bread crumbles as my lips curl around it, and Lincoln laughs, reaching out to grab a piece that fell onto my lap, bringing it to his mouth for a taste.

My thighs clench as I watch his lips wrap around his fingers—and I'm no better than a man, my salacious thoughts running rampant.

He nods to the beachside coffee shop not too far away. "Pick your poison, Gen. I'll go grab us some drinks."

"Surprise me with a festive latte." I choke, my mouth suddenly dry—and I know it's not from the sweet bread.

"Not a margarita?" he teases, shielding his eyes from the sun.

"It's not even ten!" I take another bite, then abandon it on top of the box. Pulling out the reindeer-shaped glasses, I slide them on my face like they'll do something to help shield the sun. "Better hurry, Doctor Hottie. I can't be the only jolly one here on the beach."

He quirks a brow, looking down at the hunter green long-sleeve flannel he's wearing. "I count this as festive."

A laugh bubbles from me. *Did I know he had a sarcastic humor?* "Whatever you say, buddy."

Laughing, he treks through the sand toward the coffee shop. Tiny grains scatter with every step, flying into the air as I watch him go, unable to take my eyes off him.

How the heck did I end up in his bed last night? And wake up there this morning? I must be dreaming.

Not only that, he stopped by my place before taking me to his so I could check on Pebbles. There were a few things I needed to do to make sure she was settled for the night before promptly scheduling my pet sitter to tend to her this morning.

Before our next stop on the Christmas tour, I need to stop by and check on her again.

Should I introduce her to Lincoln?

Oh my God, Genesis, she's a dog!

I'm mentally battling myself on when is the appropriate timeframe to introduce a new...suitor...to a pet, when Lincoln drops back onto the blanket next to me, handing me a to-go cup. A stream of peppermint-scented steam wafts in front of me, and I take a long, delicious sip.

"So, queen of the elves, what's on the agenda for our belated Christmas adventure today?" He nudges my shoulder with his, then brings his cup to his lips.

"How do you take your coffee?" I blurt, wanting to know so I can catalogue it for the next time we have coffee together.

I want to know everything about him, but I'll start with the simple things.

"Black, mostly. Sometimes if I'm feeling spicy, I'll add half and half and a dash of cinnamon."

I thought I caught faint notes of cinnamon on him. "Feeling spicy today?"

A mischievous glint sparks in his eyes. "A bit."

Leaning forward, he nips at my neck, dropping playful kisses and teasing bites along the column. A content sigh slips from me as I lean into him, but then I give his chest a small shove, remembering I'm supposed to be telling him about our day.

I can't be trusted around him anymore, not after last night at the holiday party. It's been on constant replay in my mind—I've never had sex in public, and even though we technically were alone, it could have taken a split second for that to change.

It was exhilarating, and as I look around the beach, I briefly wonder if we could get away with doing it here. *Briefly* being the key word as I shake the thought. Even with less than half a dozen families around, privacy is nonexistent.

Picking up my concha again, I feed him a bite. "Have you ever been to Safari Park?" I ask innocently, like I don't have the next several hours planned out. "Their Christmas tree is amazing."

Lincoln shakes his head, his mouth too full to speak.

Grinning, I pull the second pair of reindeer glasses out of the bag and slip them onto his face. "Good! That's stop two."

Chapter Fourteen

GENESIS

I'm giddy as I pull into the staff lot ten minutes early for my scheduled shift at the hospital.

Yesterday was a fairytale. Our Christmas adventure was the perfect first date, and ending the night with the sparkling displays of lights in Escondido was everything I didn't know I needed. Unfortunately, we said goodbye when he brought me home—he had to be up early to be at the hospital—but the kiss he left me with...

I fear my toes are permanently curled.

By now, Lincoln's likely on his first break of the day, and I can't help but wonder if I'll catch a glimpse of him before I check in for my rotations.

I can't believe that in less than forty-eight hours I've turned into a lust-sick puppy, clinging onto his every word and craving his presence like it's the air I breathe.

I guess this is what they call the honeymoon phase —the beginning of a blooming relationship, shiny and new.

Except Lincoln and I haven't had the relationship talk, yet. In fact, there's been no mention of whether this thing between us is casual and fun, or if it has the potential to grow into more. He openly told me one of the reasons for him avoiding me was because he was afraid if we didn't work out, it would affect Miller and Zee's relationship, and while I completely understand his hesitation, I hope he won't let it continue to drive his choices.

He and I could develop into something beautiful, but it takes two people to want to share a relationship, and if he doesn't...well, that's a reality I'll have to accept.

Stepping off the elevator, I head to the nurses' station to check in and grab my rotation schedule for the day. The desk is quiet, but as I flip through a patient's chart, the air shifts—electrifies—as the sound of footsteps approaches.

Glancing over my shoulder, I bite my lip when I see Lincoln sauntering up behind me in his white doctor's coat and blue scrubs, looking cool as a cucumber with his hands in his pockets.

"Good morning, Nurse Nikolaou." He looks up and down the hall before wrapping his arms around my waist, pulling me flush against him. "You've been on my mind." His lips trail soft kisses down my neck.

My breathing hitches, and I rest my hand over his, leaning my head against his shoulder. "I could say the same."

"Spend the night tonight." It's not a question—it's a command. Just the thought of spending another night in his bed spikes my pulse.

But I can't leave Pebbles again.

From down the hall, the elevator pings. Instinctively, we pull apart quickly, not wanting to get caught.

I round the desk, sinking into the chair, while Lincoln leans against the counter casually, pretending to read the file I abandoned.

"Doctor Stokes, have you checked in on the patient in room 602?" My eyes snap to his, voice lowering. "Come to mine instead. You can meet Pebbles."

Nurse Edwin comes into view, smiling from ear to ear as she approaches the desk. "Good morning, Doctor Stokes! Nurse Nikolaou!"

"Good morning," I greet just as cheerfully, forcing myself to focus on her, not Lincoln.

She busies herself with another stack of patient files, and Lincoln clears his throat. "I'll check on that patient, Nurse Nikolaou. Thank you. I look forward to meeting her later."

Pushing off the counter, he straightens his coat and winks at me before disappearing down the hall.

"Doctor Stokes is in a good mood today," Nurse Edwin muses, not missing a beat.

I fight the smile tugging at my lips and reach for the tablet I'll be using during my rounds today. Shaking off all thoughts of Lincoln, I wish Nurse Edwin a lovely day and head down the hall to my first patient's room.

The rest of the morning is normal—productive, even, but everywhere I go, Lincoln is there. Passing me in the hallway, standing too close as we share an elevator. The only time he's not around is when I'm with a patient or hiding in the nurses' locker room.

Yes, I'm hiding from him.

I have to—the amount of times I've wanted to fling myself onto him and kiss him senseless is embarrassing at this point.

When I finally have time to sit and take my lunch, I grab it from my locker and head down to the cafeteria. There's an empty table in the corner, and it looks like the perfect place to decompress a little.

Pulling my phone from my pocket, I scroll through my mountain of unread messages, opening the conversation with Zee. Four texts await, each getting more irritated in nature.

COME AGAIN?

You can NOT drop a bomb saying "I spent the night with Lincoln" and follow it up with SILENCE.

Miller just confirmed what you said is true. YOU SLEPT OVER AT LINCOLN'S? HOW DARE YOU LEAVE ME ON READ.

I'm going to assume you're either dead or at work, and I swear if it's not the former I'm going to put you in the hospital myself and make you wish you were six feet under. BECAUSE WHAT DO YOU MEAN YOU SLEPT AT LINCOLN'S? DID YOU SLEEP WITH LINCOLN?

"Care for some company?" Lincoln startles me, and I slam my phone down against the table so he can't see the messages from Zee. "Whoa, Gen. Everything okay?"

"Peachy!" My voice comes out in an overexaggerated squeak, like Ross from *Friends* when he's trying to convince everyone he's fine.

His brows furrow as he pulls out the chair across from me, settling into it. "How's your day going?"

"You should know," I tease. "You've been following me everywhere."

His arms cross over his chest, and he leans back. "I can't help it if you're assigned to my floor today."

"Mmm," I murmur. "Is that what we're calling it now?"

Lincoln stands abruptly, pulling his chair next to mine. My eyes widen a fraction, looking around the bustling cafeteria.

"Lincoln—" I warn, but it doesn't come out very stern.

His hand finds my knee under the table, gripping it. "Would you prefer we refer to it as something else?"

"Someone will see—"

"And?"

My breath catches in my throat. This is walking a thin line, and we both know it. But I can't help but to lean in.

A hint of a smile touches his lips as he slides his hand up just a little higher toward my thigh.

"On-call room, fifth floor. Fifteen minutes." Standing, he pushes in his chair and winds his way through the tables, stopping to say hello to a few people—both nurses and family members of patients—on his way out.

A rush of excitement bursts through me, and as calmly as I can, I stand, throw away my uneaten food, and *try* not to run out of the cafeteria to follow him.

It takes me less than ten minutes to make it to the on-call room, and thankfully, the hallway seems to be abandoned.

My palms are sweaty as I pace in front of the door, trying to convince myself this isn't the worst idea ever. As a first year nurse, I know this could jeopardize my career. Not only is sleeping with a superior highly frowned upon, and most likely against hospital policy, sleeping with them at work is practically handing HR grounds to fire me.

I'm about to change my mind, when the door opens. Leaning against the frame, Lincoln crosses his arms over his chest. "I can hear you pacing from in here."

"I guess the room isn't very soundproof then."

Tossing his head back, he laughs, then reaches for my wrist, tugging me inside.

The door clicks shut behind me, and the second we're secluded, Lincoln's hot lips are on me. Grabbing my hip, he presses me against the door.

"This is a bad idea." I groan against his lips, melting into him.

His other hand glides down my arm, lifting it by the wrist to press against the wall over my head. Leaning his hips against me, he pins me in place. "The worst."

"We're at work," I moan as his hard length rubs against my stomach. His tongue tangles with mine, and I grab a handful of his shirt, using my free hand to pull him closer.

"We are," he groans, the vibration rumbling through

our kiss. "Tell me to stop, Gen. You have the power here."

Sliding my hand up his body, I wrap it around the back of his neck, pulling him closer. "*Don't* stop."

My words snap something inside him, and the kiss changes from soft and urgent to *hungry* and frantic. Untucking my shirt, he claws at the fabric, tugging it up until he's forced to break the kiss so he can pull it over my head.

He shrugs his coat off next, then loosens his necktie, making quick work of tossing it to the side before removing his button down. As he connects our mouths again, he reaches behind me and locks the door.

Both of his hands grip my waist, fingers biting into the exposed skin just above my scrub pants. Walking backward, he pulls me with him until he's seated on the stiff bed and I'm standing between his widened legs.

Leaning forward, he kisses my stomach and pulls my pants down, taking my panties with them.

Kicking off my shoes, I step out of everything I'm wearing, now naked in front of him.

"You're so damn beautiful, Gen." His fingers dip between my legs, parting me and exploring my arousal. "I can't wait to be inside of you again."

With one hand, he pulls his scrub pants down, his thick cock springing out, eager to join the party.

Placing his hands firmly on either side of my hips again, he guides me over him, pulling me lower until my center meets his length.

"I want every piece of you, Gen," Lincoln rumbles against my collarbone, licking and nipping at it. "Anything you'll give me."

Wrapping my hand around his length, I guide it to me, pressing down an inch. "You can have all of me."

We groan in unison, his fingers digging into me harder. As he pulls me down onto him more, I open my legs further, my knees sliding against the scratchy knit blanket. Then I sink down until I've taken him completely, his length stretching me at this new angle.

Catching me in a kiss again, he begins to guide my movements, sliding my hips forward and back so I'm riding him slowly.

Bracing my hands on his shoulders, I toss my head back in pleasure and find a rhythm that has us both panting.

One thing I love about sex with Lincoln is he's *vocal*. He's not afraid to moan, to whisper my name, and to use words to encourage me.

A layer of sweat coats our bodies, the old, worn down bed squeaking beneath us. It rattles against the wall, and for a brief moment, I worry someone walking by will hear us, but as quickly as I have the thought, it's gone, lost to the pleasure.

Moving his hand between my thighs, Lincoln finds my clit. "Should we see how many times I can make you come before we have to leave this room?"

A gasp gets caught in my throat as he thrusts upward. "Not here. We have to get back."

"Nonsense. I've got all the time in the world."

"We're on the clock." My eyes roll back when his fingers begin to strum the sensitive nerve, spurring me to ride him harder.

Clenching around him, I milk his cock, sliding slowly up until barely the tip remains inside of me, then slowly pressing down until I reach the hilt.

"Fuck, Gen. I love when you do that." He works my clit harder, rolling it beneath two fingers as he applies pressure.

My body convulses. "Lincoln, I'm going to come."

Sucking hard on my neck, he licks it gently after. "Do it, baby. Let the hospital hear how sexy you sound when you're coming on my cock."

Oh my God.

His words are my undoing. My vision blurs, and a chat of illicit curses tumble from my lips. Trembling, the wave of pleasure hits continuously, crashing into me as it takes me higher.

I'm not sure I'll ever come down.

I'm not sure I want to.

I still in Lincoln's arms, our heavy breaths mingling for several heavy seconds. My chest is tight, and despite the euphoria my body's humming with, I'm finding it hard to breathe.

Lincoln's hands cup either side of my face, tilting me to look at him. "What's wrong?" His voice is filled with concern as he uses his thumbs to wipe away tears I didn't realize I had. "Gen, look at me."

An onslaught of emotions swirls through me, clouding my mind even more so than it already is.

How do I explain to him that even though we just had mind-blowing sex in the on-call room, all I can think about is this ending.

I squeeze my eyes shut.

"Gen," he consoles, wiping my tears as he leans forward and gently kisses my temple.

"This is too good to be true," I finally mutter, hiccupping between the half-whispered words.

His head shakes with vigor. "It's not."

"It *is*."

Wrapping his arms around my middle, he holds me close. "I know this is just the beginning of something for us, but I can say this with certainty. I am not a man who's ever wanted to be in a relationship before. I've been content being on my own, enjoying the occasional fling. No one has ever made me want *more*." He dips his head, catching my gaze. "*You* make me want more, Gen. I know this is crazy because it is happening so quickly, but in a sense it's also been a slow moving process between us. Now we're just making up for lost time."

"Do you mean that?" I hate how heavily the doubt weighs on my chest, and resent the neediness in my tone.

"I have no idea what the future holds—for us, or in general. We both know that anything can change in a single heartbeat, but that doesn't negate how I feel or what I want. As long as we're on the same page, I won't let anything stand in our way."

Another tear rolls down my cheek that he chases with a kiss.

"Let me make you mine, Gen. Be my girlfriend."

I'm nodding when he grabs my chin, tilting my head up to press his lips softly against mine.

And this time, when he puts my mind at ease, he does it with his body and soul, letting the words he's already spoken swirl between us until they embed themselves in my heart.

Chapter Fifteen

LINCOLN

New Year's Eve

If you'd asked me six days ago what I was doing for New Year's Eve, I would have told you absolutely nothing.

That was my plan. Quiet evening at home, by myself. Probably on call because inevitably I'll be needed at some point tonight.

But six days ago, Genesis Nikolaou turned my life upside down. Now, if you ask me what I'm doing tonight, I'll tell you I'm ringing in the New Year with my *girlfriend*.

When I step off the elevator onto Gen's floor, I can smell the cinnamon wafting through the air before I even make it down to her apartment.

Rapping my knuckles against the door, I hear light music playing behind it, and I picture her in the kitchen, dancing happily as she prepares whatever she's surprising us with.

Gen insisted she cook dinner for me, Zee, and Miller, who will be here in about an hour. She said it would be casual, followed by game night, but something in my gut tells me she's pulled out all the stops.

If there's one thing I can say with certainty, it's that she *loves* to celebrate.

Moments later when the door swings open, I'm face to face with the woman who continuously steals my breath away.

Holding a mixing bowl in one hand with a wooden spoon still buried in whatever's inside, she's wearing a dark green sweater dress, leggings, and dark gray fuzzy socks pulled up. Her wild curls are pulled back into a messy bun she's tied off with her favorite red sequined bow, and there's a smear of flour on her face.

Her apartment smells delicious, but more importantly, she *looks* delicious.

There's no way I'll make it through tonight without tasting *her*.

"Hey," she greets, a smile pulling wide across her face.

My chest tightens, squeezing my heart so tightly I'm

afraid it might burst. *Fuck, I'm falling hard for this woman.* "Hey, beautiful."

Stepping over the threshold, I kiss her cheek and am barely pulling back when Pebbles comes barreling out of the living room, her giant limbs skidding across the laminate flooring.

Slamming against my legs, she licks me in greeting, her slobbery jowls dripping, barely missing my shoe.

"Pebbles, ew!" Gen uses one hand to shoo her dog away, but it's no use—Pebbles and I have already become best friends.

This is only our second time meeting, but our introduction went off without a hitch.

"Hi, Pebbles." I laugh, giving her ear a scratch. She leans into me, so I continue rubbing her face.

"Quick—don't think, just answer." Gen flashes me a cheeky smile. "If I made you pick between me and Pebbles, who would you pick?"

My gaze drifts from the dog snuggling up against me to the woman who's trying so hard to suppress her laughter.

I lift my shoulders nonchalantly. "Pebbles."

"I knew it." Gen pulls the wooden spoon from her batter and points it in my direction. A dollop of dough falls onto the floor, and Pebbles lies down to lick it up.

"Can you blame me?" Pushing her apartment door closed so Pebbles doesn't escape, I stalk toward Genesis.

Taking the mixing bowl from her, I put it on the entryway table, then sink my fingers into her hips, pulling her close. My hand slides around the back of her neck, desperate to feel her soft skin. "I choose you every day."

Her cheeks flush, and she presses up on her tiptoes to kiss me. "Back atcha, Doctor Hottie." She winks and pulls away too quickly for my liking, dancing out of my arms. "I have to get these cookies in the oven. Make yourself at home."

Shrugging out of my jacket, I drape it over the back of one of her dining chairs and follow her into the kitchen.

The scent of cinnamon I smelled out in the hallway was nothing compared to the richness in Gen's kitchen. Sweet and savory twist together—spices, butter, meats, and something I can't put my finger on.

The baking sheet clanking against the oven rack draws my attention, my eyes locking on the pillowy baked good Gen's pulling out.

She slides the tray onto the open space on her stove, then grins at me from over her shoulder. "Ever try spanakopita?"

"Can't say I have. It's Greek food, right?" Standing

between her barstools, I lean against the counter, happily observing.

"You haven't lived until you've tried spanakopita! It's delicious."

"What's in it?"

"I make mine with traditional ingredients: feta, onion, spinach, and herbs, wrapped in phyllo dough." She presses her index finger against the outside of one. "Let them cool for a few minutes and then you're trying it."

"Deal. What's next? How can I help?"

"Just stand there and look handsome while I get these cookies in the oven."

As she rolls the dough into precise balls and places them on her parchment-lined baking sheet, I cling to her every word, watching as she works effortlessly.

The steady strum of my heart beats in my chest, and when she slides the cookies into the oven, then goes to wash her hands, I stalk over to her, unable to keep my hands to myself a second longer.

Pressing my hips into her backside, I skate my palms around the front of her, pulling her flush against me. Breathing her in, I trail open-mouth kisses against her exposed neck.

She moans under my touch, tossing the towel she's

holding onto the counter before she spins in my grasp, wrapping her arms around my neck.

I kiss her with abandon and reach my hand under her dress to rub her over her leggings.

"Lincoln—" she moans, saying my name like a prayer.

"Yes, baby?" I croon. Lifting her by the backs of her thighs, her legs wrap around me as I guide her to the counter, placing her on top of it.

"I need you."

"I know." I tug the hem of her sweater dress up, bunching it around her hips. "I've got you."

Gen lifts her hips to help me as I pull her leggings and panties down, securing them around her ankles. My cock hardens with a desperate need to be inside of her, straining against my jeans as I pull her roughly to the edge. A surprised squeal flies past her lips as her back hits the counter, and it takes me less than three seconds to dip under her legs, securing myself between them.

With the first swipe of my tongue against her wet, delicious arousal, her thighs tighten around my head. I've never felt more at home than I do between Gen's legs.

As my tongue continues its assault against Gen's clit, I relish in her moans. The way her hips squirm have me reaching down to palm my aching cock, but right now isn't about me. I can't wait to get inside of her later, but for now, I'm making it my mission to bring her to ruin against my tongue before this first batch of cookies is done.

Two fingers slide into her easily as I continue to flick my tongue against her clit. Curling upward, I find her G-spot and stroke it, watching as pleasure flits across her face.

My fingers never relent as her core tightens and she begins to spasm around them, crying out when her orgasm washes over her. Her juices drench my fingers, the sound audible as I continue to thrust them inside her.

But a quick glance at the timer on the oven tells me we still have plenty of time.

"Let's go." Grabbing Gen's hand, I pull her to sit, but before she's able to hop off the counter, I grab around her waist and hoist her over my shoulder.

"Go where!" She kicks her feet playfully, and her leggings and panties fall to the floor as I walk through her living room. "Lincoln, put me down!"

"You didn't think I was done with you already, did you?" My hand lands with a sharp smack against her exposed ass as we approach her bedroom door. Then I notice the strand of Christmas lights hanging over it—

unplugged—so I pull them down, letting them drag behind me as we enter her room.

"Hey! I was going to plug those in later," she whines playfully.

My foot kicks her door closed behind us, and I don't bother with the lights as I take her straight to her bed, tossing her onto it.

"I can think of a better use for them." Crawling up the bed, I straddle her body, tugging her dress up over her head. Our bodies press together—her fully naked, me fully clothed—and I grab both of her wrists as I lay her back down.

A smile tugs at my lips. Grabbing the Christmas lights I temporarily abandoned to undress her, I slowly wind them around her wrists and down her arms, securing them over her head.

"You're tying me up?" Her eyes glitter with excitement.

I unplug her phone charger and plug in the lights instead. The room instantly illuminates with soft, multi-colored lights that cast a festive glow around us.

Still holding her wrists, I lean down and kiss her hard. She watches me with a hunger in her eyes as I shed my clothes, using controlled care to remove the fabric from my body. By the time I lower myself on top of her, the room is charged with combustible electricity, both of us desperate for the other.

Gen's legs wrap around my hips, pulling me closer to her. There's no doubt in my mind that this woman was meant to be mine.

Brushing my fingers down her cheek, I kiss her softly, rolling my hips into her until we're both writhing. I sit up and look deeply into her eyes, restraining myself from devouring her.

"Gen, you'll tell me if I do anything you're not comfortable with, right?" I run a finger up her stomach, softly touching her skin. She shivers beneath me, her eyes searching mine.

"Of course. Why?"

Grabbing her hips, I flip her over, pulling her up onto all fours. Her soft moans fill the room as I slowly kiss down her spine. Bringing my hand between her legs, I push two fingers inside of her. She jolts forward at the sudden intrusion, her head dropping low on her shoulders.

"Lincoln," she moans again, and my cock twitches in appreciation.

"Fuck, the sound my name on your lips does things to me, Gen." Wrapping my hand around my cock, I align it with her entrance and push inside of her without warning. She yelps a surprised cry that quickly turns into a pleasure-filled moan. Grabbing hold of the lights wrapped around her wrists, I gently guide her arms up and over her head, forcing her back to arch.

I force her arms to stay upright, holding onto the strand that keeps them tied together, and I knead her breast with my free hand, thrusting into her relentlessly.

Moments later, our releases crash into us in a single, soul-shattering collision. I've never come so hard in my life, and for a second, all I can do is catch my breath on top of her—the rhythm of her breathing grounding me.

"Damn." She releases a shaky exhale, a smile spreading across her lips.

"You can say that again." I laugh, the intensity still lingering. It wasn't just mind-blowing sex, our connection...that was something else entirely.

I roll off her, then reach to unplug the lights, plunging us into darkness. Gently, I unwind the strand from her wrists, then toss it near the edge of the bed.

As soon as I settle against her pillow again, she intertwines our fingers. So many emotions run through my mind, but I'm not sure how to articulate them. Gen stays quiet too, and I realize at that moment, words aren't needed.

Our bodies spoke them for us.

She sighs contentedly and rolls onto her side to face me. I do the same, tucking a stray piece of her hair behind her ear. I'm about to tell her I'm falling for her when the smoke detector startles us both.

"Oh my God!" she gasps, bolting upright. "The cookies!"

"Why's it smoky here?" Zee wrinkles her nose as she walks into Gen's apartment thirty minutes later with Miller in tow.

We did our best to air out the apartment, but the second Gen started to shiver, I went around and closed the windows again.

I grin as Genesis groans. "Don't ask."

"Gen was a little tied up for a while, and we burnt a batch of cookies." The image of her wrists wrapped in Christmas lights flashes through my mind, instantly hardening me again.

Rubbing her lower back, I shift her in front of me, not needing my cousin and his girlfriend to see how the memory is currently affecting me.

"This is going to take me a second to get used to," Zee mutters, stepping further into the apartment.

Pebbles leaps from the couch and gallops over to Zee, jumping on her. She towers over Zee while on her hind legs, and Miller steadies her by placing his hand on her back as she sways.

"Hi, my girl. Auntie missed you so much," Zee coos, ruffling Pebbles's ears while the humongous dog licks her face. "Did you miss me? I missed you!"

Laughing, Gen shakes her head and busies herself as Zee and Miller settle into her apartment. I spring into action, moving around the kitchen as though it's my own.

"You two are awfully cozy," Miller observes with a playful quirk of his brow. "Can I do anything?"

"Yeah." I thrust the platter of sliced pot roast toward him. "Make yourself useful and take this to the table."

"Dick," he teases, then balances it on one hand. "Give me something else."

I pass him a gravy boat, and he tosses me a wink like he's the lead server at a Michelin star restaurant.

Dinner is lively and full of laughter. Zee fires a few hundred questions at me and Gen in rapid succession, wanting to know everything about what happened between us, where it was going, and most importantly, are we in love?

"It's only been a week!" Gen emphasizes when Zee asked the last question, her cheeks flushing as she flicks her gaze to me.

"So? Miller and I fell in love in a week," Zee says nonchalantly, popping a roasted carrot into her mouth.

"I—we—" Gen stammers.

Sliding my hand under the table, I lace our fingers together, squeezing gently. "You're the exception, Zee. Not the rule. Some people need more than a week to fall in love, but to answer your question—yes, I *do* have very strong feelings for Gen."

Our conversation quickly shifts after that to resolutions for the new year, and finally, to wedding planning.

Gen rests her head on her hand, staring dreamily at the glittering diamond settled on Zee's ring finger. Miller proposed on Christmas, and the girls have been gushing over the proposal on and off through dinner.

"So." Zee clears her throat. "We know we've only been engaged for, like, a minute, but Miller and I have something we want to ask each of you."

She looks over at Miller, who grins at his fiancée. "This may come as a shock to both of you, but you two are the most important people in each of our lives. This relationship better work out between you guys because—"

"Because we want you to be our maid of honor and best man!" Zee finishes for him, too excited to let Miller finish his sentence.

Gen shrieks with excitement, launching out of her

chair. It scrapes against the floor, toppling over, but neither of the girls notice. Her and Zee collide in an embrace, full of bouncing and squealing.

Miller and I shake our heads, then pull each other into an embrace of our own. "Of course I'll be your best man."

"Good," he says, clapping me on the back. "'Cuz I don't have a brother. Or friends. So it's you, or no one."

"Wow, I'm so honored to be your only option."

Later, when the girls have dried their tears and Miller and I have cleaned up from dinner, we get comfortable in Gen's living room with a stack of board games.

After several rounds of Cards Against Humanity, HeadBandz, and even a round of Life, Gen turns the TV on. We all stand as the pre-recorded ball drop ticks down, the last two minutes of this year vanishing before our eyes.

My heart hammers in my chest, excitement and nerves melding together. Gen leans against me, and I wrap my arms around her waist, swaying gently as we wait.

The countdown reaches thirty seconds.

Then twenty.

Zee and Miller are in their own world as they watch

the countdown. I turn Gen in my arms, guiding hers around my neck.

Kissing her softly, I let the world fade away just as I hear Zee shout, "Ten!"

"It's too fast for 'I love you's'," I whisper against her lips, "but I want you to know how much you mean to me, Genesis."

"Seven!"

"There's nothing more important to me than you, and I know it's crazy, but I mean it when I say I'll never let you go. Next year, or whenever you're ready, it'll be us asking them to be in our wedding party—"

"Four!"

"—Because make no mistake, Gen. You and I are forever."

"HAPPY NEW YEAR!"

Miller and Zee erupt into cheers, but all I hear is Gen's soft whisper of my name as tears fill her eyes.

Bending slightly, I lift her effortlessly into my arms. Her legs wrap around my hips as I cradle her.

Then I steal her first kiss of the new year, kissing her slow and deep—like a silent promise that I'll always be hers.

Like she's my beginning, my end, my forever.

Like she's already my wife.

Epilogue

GENESIS

Two Months Later

Nausea holds me in its clutches as the car winds higher up the mountain, each curve of the road churning my stomach a little more. The sun beats down on the dashboard, thickening the air around me in a stifling cocoon. Sweat beads at the back of my neck, and I lock my eyes on the road, willing the disorienting feeling to pass.

As a child, my family always had to pull off at some point during the hour drive to Julian because I could never make it the whole way without turning green.

It's great to see that as an adult, things haven't changed.

"I didn't realize you get carsick so easily." Lincoln's brows knit together as he flicks his gaze at me. "I could have had my parents come to us."

"No! I'm okay." I blow out a shaky breath. "You'd think I would have outgrown it by now."

"Some people don't." He reaches for the air vents, repositioning them so they all blow in my direction, then he cracks the windows. "Do you need me to pull over?"

I shake my head, but the sudden motion makes me queasy. "Maybe just some more air."

He cranks the air conditioner, and I fix my gaze on the road again, hoping this disgusting feeling passes quickly.

"We're almost there, I promise." Lacing his fingers through mine, Lincoln rests our hands on my thigh. "Close your eyes and rest for a while, it might help."

I do, because he's right—sleep used to be the only thing that would help, and I'm sure *that* hasn't changed either.

It seems like only a few seconds when a soft squeeze on my knee rouses me.

"We're here, baby."

Yawning, I blink awake and immediately take in the picturesque view of the Stokes family home.

Then I realize I'm not flooded with queasiness anymore—the feeling has turned into something else.

Nerves.

I'm meeting Lincoln's parents.

After two months together, we've decided it's time to meet each other's parents. Dinner last night with mine went off without a hitch. Today, we're spending a cozy day in Julian with his.

"I hope they like me," I murmur, more to myself than to Lincoln as I unbuckle.

"They're going to *love* you, Gen."

He hops out of the car and comes around to open the door for me, and before he can, his mom comes bounding down the porch steps, arms wide. "Oh my goodness, there she is!"

I'm barely standing when she pulls me into a tight hug, squeezing me like she's met me a thousand times. "Oh, sweetheart, do you have any idea how glad I am to finally meet you? I've been waiting way too long for Linc to bring someone home!"

Laughter bubbles within me, and my eyes begin to fill with tears. Mrs. Stokes squeezes me tight again before pulling back to look at me.

"You're even more beautiful than I imagined you'd be. Tim! TIM! Come meet Lincoln's girlfriend. She's lovely!"

"Mom," Lincoln chastises, steering her away from me and pulling her into his own hug. Over her shoulder, he mouths *sorry*, shaking his head. "You didn't even tell Gen your name."

"Ah! I'm just so excited. Can you blame me?" Standing up straight, she shakes out her shoulders like she's shaking off her giddiness, then extends her hand. Schooling her features, she greets me again. "Hi, I'm Tina."

I take it, laughing. "Hi Tina, it's so good to finally meet you."

"Tina, for goodness' sake, give the woman a second to stretch her legs," Lincoln's dad, Tim, grumbles from the porch. He's leaning against the railing with a steaming mug in his hand and a playful grin on his face. "Can I get you lovebirds a cup of coffee?"

"That'd be great, thanks, Dad." Lincoln laces his fingers through mine and leads me up the porch steps. Warmth surrounds me as I step inside their home, from the roar of their fireplace to the soft, delicate scent of coffee, pine, and cinnamon. As Lincoln pulls my sweater from my shoulders, I peek around at the cozy nostalgia of the home Lincoln grew up in.

Settling around the oak kitchen table, Tina buzzes around her kitchen, pulling open cabinets. "Are you guys hungry? How's brunch sound?"

Lincoln looks over at me, and I nod. "Brunch sounds perfect. How can I help?"

"By sitting there and telling me all about you!" Tina winks, then gets to work pulling out ingredients.

As Tim slides two mugs of coffee in front of us, he asks, "How do you two take your coffee? Lincoln, still black with a splash of cream?"

"Black is fine. Creamer for Gen," Lincoln answers his dad. Draping an arm around the back of my chair, he kisses my cheek.

Walking back to the refrigerator, Tim pulls out an assortment of creamers, including one that surprises me —peppermint.

Nuzzling my ear, Lincoln mutters, "I may have asked Dad to pick up an extra one before the season ended."

"Don't worry," Tim chimes in. "It's not expired; these things last forever."

Laughing, I unscrew the cap. "This is the sweetest thing anyone's ever done for me, thank you, Tim."

"Hey!" Lincoln protests. "I had a hand in that too."

It's a simple gesture that warms my heart—not only did Lincoln think of me, but his parents played a part in it without a second thought.

An hour later, after good food and even better conversation, Tina and Tim insist on cleaning everything themselves and shoo us away. Lincoln leads me to the back porch to a wooden swing overlooking the garden, where we settle in for a moment alone.

"Thank you for bringing me to meet your parents." I lean my head against his shoulder. "They're amazing."

"I told you they'd love you." He presses his lips to the top of my head. "If you couldn't tell, my mom's been waiting a long time for me to bring someone special home."

"You've never introduced her to a girlfriend before?"

He shakes his head, the movement bouncing the swing. "Not until last Christmas when I brought Zee home—but that was just a desperate attempt to have my mom *stop* urging me to settle down."

"And before that?" I look up at him, surprised. I knew he wanted to wait a while before bringing me to meet his parents, but he never explained why.

"There's never been anyone special before," Lincoln says quietly.

His eyes find mine, and behind them, I can see our entire life together, the picture streaming vividly from his thoughts to mine. He lifts our hands, pressing a kiss to the back of mine.

"I love you," he finally says softly.

I release a breathless laugh, weeks of apprehension melting away because I've been worried about falling too fast. He just said the three words aloud that I've been whispering in my head on repeat for what feels like forever.

"I love you too, Lincoln," I whisper back, feeling the truth of it throughout my whole body.

"Good." He grins brightly, and pulls me onto his lap. "I was hoping you'd say that because Mom already has a stocking with your name embroidered on it."

"It's only February." I giggle as he peppers kisses against my cheek and neck.

"Aren't you the one who's always telling me it's never too early to look forward to Christmas?" He wraps his arms tighter around me while whispering *I love you* over and over.

"Yeah." I catch his face between my fingers, gripping his cheeks softly. Our breath mingles as I close the distance between us, our lips practically touching. "I guess I am."

Then I kiss him—the man I love.

The man who loves *me*.

Last Christmas didn't feel like Christmas at all, but this year? Well, maybe Santa deserves a night off.

Thank you for reading Not Like Christmas At All! Your reviews are important, please considering leaving your review of Not Like Christmas At All on Amazon.

Ready for more from A.R. Rose?

Check out Zee and Miller's whirlwind Christmas
romance in I Really Can't Stay!

Enter into your baseball era and check out Stealing
Forever, a single dad/nanny, age gap, baseball romance!

Acknowledgments

Happy holiday's to my ho ho ho's! I hope you loved Lincoln and Gen's story as much as I enjoyed writing them. Christmas has always been my favorite holiday, and writing two San Diego based stories centered around the best time of year has been a dream.

A special thank you to YOU. Without you taking the time to read my books, none of this could be possible. YOU help me chase my dream every single day.

Thank you to Kat, Delynda, Slasher, Cassie, and Ellyn for being in my corner throughout the last few months, constantly cheering me on even when I forget how to cheer for myself.

Thank you to my editorial team for being amazing and pushing me to be more polished with every story.

Thank you to my family and friends for always being the biggest supporters in my life. I love you all so much.

And finally, an extra special thank you to all ARC readers and influencers on my team who always show their love and support.

A.R. Rose's greatest job in life is being a mom to her two boys. She is a born and raised California native who loves to hang out at home with her kids and her dog.

A.R. realized her passion for writing in the third grade, although it wasn't until early 2022 when she began to pursue it. Now, if she skips a day of writing, she feels as though her day is incomplete.

On any given day, you will find A.R. toting around her laptop and her Kindle, with a coffee in hand, daydreaming about the characters and worlds she's building. She is grateful to have the opportunity to bring her stories to life and is excited about her journey as a romance writer.

CONNECT

Join A.R. Rose's newsletter for info & updates

https://www.authorarrose.com/email-subscribe

Website

www.authorarrose.com

Reading Group

https://www.facebook.com/groups/authorarrose

Facebook

https://www.facebook.com/authorarrose

TikTok

https://www.tiktok.com/@authorarrose

Instagram

https://www.instagram.com/authorarrose

Declan

Three months ago

"I quit, Mr. Lane. I'm sorry."

"I—?" My nanny is quitting? I haven't even been home for thirty seconds. Hell, I'm not even one step inside of the front door, my heavy backpack's still slung over my shoulder and there's mud caked on the bottom of my slides that I haven't had a chance to kick off yet. "What?"

My bag hits the floor with a heavy thud, and I scrub my hands down my face in frustration, or maybe it's exhaustion. Probably both, it's been a damn day.

She pushes off the couch to her feet and folds the blanket she'd been sitting under. "I'm sorry. I know this is abrupt, but I didn't want to lose the courage. I just can't do these late nights, and I know the season is starting soon, so you'll be traveling. I'm just realizing this isn't the gig for me."

Fuck. It took me weeks to find Liza—now I'll have to start all over again.

Swallowing the lump in my throat, I nod curtly. "Understood. Any chance you have a referral for a replacement?"

A friend? A family member? *Fucking anyone?*

"I'll put some feelers out. I'm *really* sorry, Mr. Lane."

"It's fine," I grumble. It's not fine, but what else am I supposed to say?

She bends over in front of me to pick up her purse by the door, and I avert my eyes, glancing around my living room instead.

"What time did she go to sleep?" A glance at my watch tells me it's nearing eleven. No wonder Liza is quitting—I told her I'd be home by nine. She isn't a live-in nanny, and I'm sure my constant tardiness drives her crazy. In my defense, I warned her prior to her taking the job.

She smiles, shifting her hand to curl around the strap of her bag as she readies herself to leave. "Seven-thirty sharp. I did a load of her laundry earlier, but didn't wash her stuffed animals since she wanted to sleep with Snug-Bug. I also bought new berries at the market today, and they're washed and ready in the fridge. Your credit card is on the counter."

"Thank you, Liza."

"No problem. Sorry things didn't work out on my end."

"I understand." Do I, though? She's only been with us for two months. Sure, my time management sucks, but when she interviewed to nanny for a single dad she should have known. Unfortunately, things have been a lot busier than I anticipated they'd be when I hired her, but I'm gearing up for my first year as *head coach*.

And although I'm no spring chicken at thirty-six years old, I'm the youngest the Bridge Point Bears have ever had. Which is why I've been pulling such long hours to prove myself, not only to the managerial staff, but to my team.

Because goddamn, do I have my work cut out for me with these guys.

Opening the front door, I hold it for her. "Thanks for everything."

"Please tell Sailor I said bye." She gives me a small wave, then walks out the front door, never once looking back.

I watch and make sure she makes it safely into her car parked on the street, then shut the door. Slumping against it, I mutter a curse.

Finding a nanny to work for a single dad is hard enough—I know what it's like for women these days, and I don't fault them for being leery of men.

Hell, if I were female, I'd be cautious, too. So the second they learn there is no missus, half of the candidates lose interest in scheduling an interview to meet me and my three-year-old daughter.

Then, it's a game of Goldilocks to find the right fit for us.

I *really* don't want to go through this again, but I have no other choice.

Sailor deserves far more than a revolving door of babysitters, she deserves someone who loves her and will give her the best care, day in and day out, when that person can't be me.

And I'm determined to find the perfect woman for the job, no matter what.

"C'mon, Sailor, Daddy's going to be late!" The clock on the wall taunts me, reminding me we should have left ten minutes ago. My meeting with the Bears' execs is in less than thirty minutes, and I need to make it across Bridge Point in the next twenty.

"But I want Snug-Bug!" Sailor stomps her little foot on the ground, her arms crossed with a sour look on her face.

"Snug-Bug *just* went into the dryer, Sail. He'll be nice and clean by the time we get home."

Her eyes fill with tears, and she gives me the goddamn pouty lip that makes my heart tear to shreds every single time.

"How about a cookie?" I scoop her up, succumbing to bribery. With Sailor on my hip, I open the pantry and use one hand to pop the lid on the plastic container full of Oreos. Her little grabby hands swipe it from me, so I grab another, sticking it between my teeth, then shift one to the hand I'm holding her with.

With Sailor distracted, I bolt to the front door, stopping only to pick up my backpack and lock the house up. When I've finally wrangled my daughter into her car seat, I haul ass through town—safely of course, but as fast as I can.

She isn't *supposed* to come with me, but since my nanny quit last night, my only option is to bring her.

The sound of *Ms. Rachel* floats through the car from her tablet, and I hope to God the device keeps her busy during this meeting.

Today is not a day for no screen time.

Traffic is light, thankfully, and I pull into a parking

spot adjacent to the stadium and hang my parking permit with minutes to spare. It leaves me enough time to get us into the conference room that overlooks the ballpark.

Depositing her into a leather office chair that engulfs her tiny frame, I prop her tablet in her lap, lay her favorite blanket next to her, and hand her the last Oreo. She doesn't even look up at me by the time I've frantically situated her, but I can't say the same for the audience I now have.

When I take my seat, all eyes are on me.

Considering this is only my second meeting with the executives, my heart is hammering. Hopefully, I'm not canned for bringing my kid.

"You brought your kid?" Blake Bradley, the team's owner, scoffs, ironically echoing my thoughts. His eyes scrutinize me, but I hold my head high. He's not much older than I am, but he's the one looking out of place, wearing a three-piece suit at a ballpark. Fuckin' billionaires.

"My nanny quit on me last night." I lean back, draping my arm over the armrests of mine and Sailor's chairs.

"Oof. That's a toughy." Clive, the team's accountant, taps his pen against the lined-yellow notepad in front of him.

"I'll find another." *Eventually.* I'm not holding out hope that this will be a speedy process.

The conversation gets cut short when Blake begins speaking about the upcoming season, potential trades, and finances.

Around the oblong conference table sit the most important men behind the scenes for the Bridge Point Bears: the owner, the in-house lawyers, our accountant, and, of course, the coaches, myself as the head coach *and* manager, and my four assistant coaches.

Our team is the strongest we've ever been *behind-the-scenes*, and if we secure the trades Blake's hoping we do, we'll be a force on the field as well.

For years, the Bears have been the underdogs in the majors, but since Blake Bradley bought the team two years ago, things have been looking up significantly. With loads of cash at his disposal, he's dumped it into higher salaries, better trade offers, and incredible upgrades to an already brand new stadium.

My promotion came at the perfect time, and I'm grateful for the previous coach's glowing recommendation prior to retirement. I was a shoo-in, having worked for the Bears since I was eighteen. Baseball's been my life since I was four and started Little League. It's in my blood. In my DNA.

I eat, sleep, and *breathe* baseball.

Just being a player for the Bears, or any other team, would've never been enough for me.

I wanted it *all*. I wanted to coach. Be the *head coach*.

And now I am.

An hour and a half, and a pissed off three-year-old later, we're all clearing the room, done for the day.

"Hey, Lane, you got a moment?" Clive pushes his wire-framed glasses further up his nose, stepping around the table closer to me.

"That's not Daddy's name. Daddy's name is Declan." Sailor's nose scrunches, then she looks back down at her tablet, now blaring *Bluey*.

Clive chuckles, shifting his shoulder bag while smiling down at my girl. "Yes, yes, you're right, little one. Sometimes we call your dad by your last name, though." His eyes meet mine. "I might have an answer to your nanny problem."

"Oh?" My backpack hits my shoulders roughly as I toss it on, listening while preparing to leave.

"Why?" Sailor looks up at Clive with confusion. I pick her up and settle her in my arms.

The old man smiles in amusement at Sailor, then shifts his gaze back to me. "I recently rented one of my townhouses to a young woman who's getting her masters through Ridgewood U. Very sweet gal. She mentioned how she wanted to find a job working with kids, since her degrees are in education. She currently works in retail. Anyway, I could contact her to see if she'd babysit for you."

"I really need more of a nanny than a babysitter. You know how grueling the on-season schedule can be."

Clive swishes his hand in my direction as he looks down the curve of his nose to his phone's screen. He roughly taps a few times before bringing it to his ear.

"You're calling her *now*?" I shift Sailor's weight and use my other hand to adjust my backpack.

"No better time than the present—oh! Hi, Hailey. How are you?" He listens intently, nodding as the woman talks.

I know absolutely nothing about this girl. Not her name—although, I guess it's Hailey—her age, or if she even lives in Bridge Point.

"Clive, it's fine. I can just put out an ad," I gruffly whisper, embarrassment flickering through me.

He ignores me. "Glad to hear it. I'm thrilled you're settling in. Hey—question. You'd said you wanted to work with the youngsters. Any interest in being a nanny?"

It feels like time halts while we both wait for her response, although I can't hear their conversation.

A smile breaks out on Clive's face. "That's wonderful! The coach for the Bears is looking for someone to help with his daughter. Hold on, I'll put you on speaker." He jams his finger against the screen, then holds the device flat on his palm. "Hailey, I have Declan here. Let me catch him up to speed."

Because the conversation is so complex?

"Hailey said she loves to work with kids and is interested in talking to you more about watching Sailor."

"Hey, Declan," Hailey's soft and sensual voice flits through the phone. It stirs something inside of me that I immediately ignore.

"Hi, Hailey. I'm so sorry, Clive and I are catching you off guard."

"No worries at all! So you're in the market for a nanny? How old is your daughter?"

"Sailor is three. She goes to preschool a couple days a week, but my hours with the team are all over the place, and I could use the extra help." I *don't* tell her my last nanny quit on me because she hated my inconsistent schedule. "Clive mentioned you're getting your masters, though, and I, uh—"

On instinct, my fingers sweep through my overgrown hair. Fuck, this suddenly feels incredibly awkward.

Hailey laughs, probably sensing the tension radiating off me through the phone. "My classes are all online, so an unpredictable schedule is not a problem."

"Okay, great. It's probably a good idea for you to

come to the house, then we can discuss everything, and you can get a feel for Sailor. See if it's a good fit."

Glancing up, my eyes meet Clive's again. He has a wide smile on his face and nods enthusiastically, giving a thumbs-up.

For some inexplicable reason, my chest tightens when I look back down at the phone, completely unaware that less than ten words would be the start of life as I know it changing forever.

"Sure! I'd love to meet you both. How's tomorrow?"

Chapter One

Hailey

"No, wait! Don't grab that, it's—"

The bag of flour hits the kitchen floor with a heavy *crash*, going everywhere, and leaving the air clouded in an explosion of hazy white.

"—going to fall." Sighing, I bend over to pick up a now crying Sailor. Her thumb immediately goes into her mouth for comfort as I pat her back. "It's okay, it was an accident."

Flour is *everywhere*—a full Costco-sized ten-pound bag more than half emptied on the tile. Sailor's covered in it, as am I, and I know it's going to be a disaster to clean.

"C'mon, let's get you into the tub." The cookies can wait. So can the mess.

Turning off the oven, the sounds of keys rattling in the lock pull my attention to the front door. *Of course he's home early, the* one *night.*

Seconds later, my boss's face comes into view as he steps into the house. He's wearing his Bears T-shirt and hat, with his overgrown hair peeking past the sides, and a heavy backpack thrown over his shoulder. He takes that thing everywhere.

When Declan Lane sees his daughter and me, his grin slips as his eyes rake over us. "What happened?"

Tossing his keys into a basket, he drops his bag before stalking toward us, hands outstretched when he's a couple steps away. Sailor pulls from me and reaches for her dad, nuzzling in his arms when he takes her. Flour transfers, clinging to his black shirt.

"We had a bit of an accident." Embarrassed, I brush my shirt, trying but failing to make myself more presentable. "We were making cookies and the bag of flour took a tumble..."

"Oh no." Declan's eyes widen at Sailor, a smile pulling at the corners of his mouth. "Is the kitchen a big mess?"

She nods her head yes, still sucking her thumb. Gently, he pulls it from her mouth. We've been working together to try and break her of the habit.

"That's okay." He kisses the side of her head. "Accidents happen. Do you want me to give you a bath, or Ms. Hailey?"

"Ms. Hailey," Sailor tells him, shimmying against his hold. He places her on the floor, and she comes back to me and takes my hand. Pride settles in my chest at the simple gesture that means so much.

Before I started working for the Lane family, I was terrified Declan's daughter would be a nightmare, or wouldn't bond with me. There's a reason why his past nanny quit, right? Although the conversation never came up, I'm not daft enough to think I'm the first nanny he's hired.

"I'll clean up the kitchen when I'm finished," I promise Declan as I lead Sailor through their living room.

His only response is a grunt, but that's nothing new. Declan is a good man and an excellent father from what I've seen, but he's not overly chatty. Typically, by the time he gets home, he looks like he's exhausted.

Once I have Sailor bathed and in her jammies, I settle her on the couch and put a movie on, then ready myself to deal with the mess in the kitchen.

Only, when I step around the counter island, the floor is spotless. In fact, the whole kitchen is completely clean.

A beeping catches me off guard, causing me to jump, slamming my hand against my chest. Turning, I realize Declan put the cookies in the oven.

My heart flips.

Pulling them out, I transfer the delicious treats onto a metal cooling rack before sliding the next batch in.

When I turn around, Declan's leaning against the wall, his arms crossed over his chest, watching me. His hair is a mess from wearing a hat all day, curling around his ears, and he's filthy—his T-shirt and jeans have dirt—and now flour—clinging to them.

Swallowing hard, I avert my gaze and pretend that I'm not insanely interested in him, and turn to clean a non-existent messy spot on the counter.

I shouldn't be this attracted to him. For one, he's eleven years older than me. *And* he's my boss. *And* a single dad. And my *boss*.

"You didn't have to clean up this giant mess." My voice is a lot breathier than it should be as I scrub the already sparkling stove. "I had planned to after Sailor's bath."

"I know, but you've been with her all day. It wasn't a problem."

"You worked all day," I counter. Glancing over my shoulder, I notice he's now leaning against the island, leaning on his forearms. His gaze is dropped to his phone lying on the marble, and whatever he's looking at is making his brows furrow.

Once again, I try not to stare.

I've worked for Declan for almost three months now, and I still haven't built an immunity against his charm. The pathetic thing is, he's not even trying to be charming. He just is.

Even if I was interested in him, which I'm *not*, I'm not his type.

I've seen photos of Sailor's mom. She's stunning. Petite. Brunette. Tanned skin and chocolate brown eyes. A smile that I just know lights up every room she walks in.

Literally my opposite in every way.

I'm curvy, with flaming red hair, pale skin, and green eyes. I love myself, don't get me wrong, but I know I'm not his cup of tea.

But again, I'm *not* interested in my boss.

"Fucking idiots," Declan mumbles before locking his screen. Pushing it off to the side, he turns his attention my way. "Technically, you're off the clock when I get home, Hailey. The least I can do is help out when I'm here."

"It was a big mess though. So, thank you."

"It was. Pretty sure you two shouldn't be allowed to

bake again. If this is what happens when there are cookies, I can't imagine what the kitchen would look like if you girls baked a cake," he teases, and I almost drop the plate in my hand. This is a side to Declan Lane I've never seen before.

Setting the plate in front of him, he grabs a warm chocolate chip cookie, and I shrug. "You won't be saying that after you taste my cookie."

Once the words leave my mouth, I realize I could have chosen better ones. And Declan must realize that, too, because he chokes on said cookie, coughing aggressively.

Heat instantly rises in my skin, embarrassment taking root throughout my entire body.

For several awkward seconds, we simply stare at each other. Then the bastard starts *laughing*.

Kill me. Just kill me now.

Spinning as quickly as possible, I busy myself cleaning up the last part of the kitchen by crumpling the used parchment and throwing it away, then sliding the baking sheet into the drawer under the oven. Declan's hot gaze follows me throughout each movement—I *feel* it, and if I had the ability to melt into a puddle and evaporate, I would. Or I could live out my days as a puddle, too. *Anything* would be better than feeling this heat slither up my neck and onto my face as Declan's hot gaze bores into me. I don't dare turn around and show him how embarrassed I truly am.

I got to get out of here.

"Okay, well, I'll leave you to it!" Springing into action, I toss the towel onto the counter, mentally calculating how quickly I can make it to the front door.

"Hailey, wait." Declan's still laughing, and even though now my back's to him, I scrunch my nose and wave my hand in a weird and hasty departure.

Next to the door, I'm practically falling over as I bounce on one foot, tugging my sneaker onto the other. As I lose balance, my palm slams into the wall.

"Get home safe." Declan's low timbre sneaks up on me from behind, and I suck in a breath. He's so close, I can feel the heat from his body and his breath as it dusts the back of my neck.

For a second, I think he's about to wrap me in his arms, and I forget how to breathe. All I can do is stand still. I squeeze my eyes shut, and wonder if he can hear the gallop of my fight-or-flight heart.

Then, like a movie being unpaused, everything around us snaps back to reality—the blare of the show Sailor's watching, her adorable laugh, the ringing of Declan's phone in the kitchen.

He reaches around me, and twists the doorknob

before moving his hand to grip the door, holding it open for me.

Blowing out a shaky breath, I glance up at him from over my shoulder. The look on his face is inexpressive—maybe even a little bored.

My heart sinks.

"Thanks," I mutter, then grab my purse from the bottom shelf of the entryway table and hightail it out the door.

Once I'm in my car, I glance back at the house to make sure Declan is out of view, then slam my head against the headrest. "Stupid, stupid, stupid."

Squeezing my eyes shut for a second, I scoff at myself, shaking my head.

You won't be saying that after you taste my cookie. You utter freaking moron.

Even in the darkness of my car, embarrassment heats my cheeks *again*.

After I've given the engine a few minutes to warm up, I make the drive back to my townhouse, about twenty minutes away.

Bridge Point has bloomed over the last few years, going from a city in need of a serious glow-up to a popular destination, its biggest draw being Coit Stadium and the Bears moving in. Having Ridgewood as a neighbor helped too, since the university brings over the college students.

Which is what brought me to town last year. I needed a change of scenery from Southern California, and decided to pursue my masters in education at Ridgewood U. I landed in Bridge Point simply for the slightly more affordable housing, then decided to do this semester fully online.

It's better that way, considering my new position with the Lane family.

Oh, God.

My mind floats back to the look on Declan's face.

Pressing my twin sister's name on my car's screen, the phone begins to ring obnoxiously loud through the speakers, assaulting my eardrums until she answers.

"Hey," Hartley greets me. Just hearing her voice sends calming frequencies through my body. I miss her so much.

Hartley and I are fraternal twins, although no one ever believes us because we're so different, both physically and in personality.

I groan at my sister dramatically. "My words didn't word properly again. I'm so embarrassed, Hart."

Her laughter fills the car. "Oh no, now what'd you say? And to who?"

"Who do you think?"

"You embarrassed yourself in front of your smokin' hot boss, didn't you?"

"Yup." I pop the p on purpose. "Start digging a hole."

"For your body or his?"

"Mine, because I've already died from humiliation. In fact, I'm speaking to you from beyond the grave."

Hartley exhales a laugh, and I can practically hear her eye roll. "Sorry. Can't. I love you too much, plus I'm not made for manual labor."

"Of course not. Much too lithe for that. How's rehearsals going?"

"No, no. Don't deflect," Hartley scolds. "What'd you say to your boss?"

"I made chocolate chip cookies, which he ended up baking for me because Sailor and I made a giant mess and I needed to get her cleaned up. But then, when I took them out of the oven, he joked and said something like 'you shouldn't be allowed to bake' and I said something like 'you haven't tasted my cookie yet.'"

There's a rustling behind the receiver, and as I slow for a red light, I white-knuckle my steering wheel, anticipating her response.

"What's so bad abou—oh. OH. *Hailey!*" Hartley's laughter fills the car so boisterously, I turn the volume down. She doesn't stop laughing until the light turns green and I'm about to turn into my neighborhood.

"You can stop laughing now."

"Only you could turn *that* into something more. Did he even put two and two together?"

"Of course he did. *Immediately.*"

"What was his reaction?"

"Same as yours. I should quit, right? That's the only natural progression to this."

"You better not! You love working for him."

"*Loved.* Past tense. I loved working for him before I made an ass of myself." The repetitive click of my blinker competes against my words.

"Oh, stop. It'll all be blown over by tomorrow."

"When are you coming to see me?" I ask, putting my car in park. I leave it running, though, so I can finish talking to my sister. "I miss you, Hart."

"I know, I miss you too. I think the Rebels play the Bears here next month. Will you be flying down? Or are you stuck up in Bridge Point with the kiddo?"

"I'm coming down! There's going to be a few games, so Declan wants me and Sailor to come so he can still spend time with her when they're not on the field."

"I still can't believe you ended up with a nanny job for the Bears coach. What are the odds we both end up connected to a baseball team in some capacity?"

"It's pretty funny considering dad's a football guy through and through."

"Now we're wearing jerseys for the wrong sports."

"Technically, you're the only one wearing a jersey. I'm wearing mac and cheese stains and flour on a T-shirt."

"Ew."

"Mmhmm. Alright, I just pulled into my driveway and need to go shower–I'm still covered in flour. I love you. Thanks for making me feel better."

"Always a phone call away."

"And a short plane ride," I singsong the end of our mantra to her. It's the only thing that got us through the first couple months being separated for the first time *ever*. "I'll see you next month."

When the call disconnects, I turn my car off and grab my purse from the passenger seat, watching my surroundings as I exit my car and head for the house. You can never be too careful.

When I'm inside, I don't bother turning the lights on and instead, drop my bag at my feet and schlep through the darkness up the stairs, ready to wash off the evidence of the day.

The mac and cheese.

Sailor's snot residue.

The flour.

And most importantly, the freaking embarrassment that's rooted into my mind.

And clothing.

All of it can wash down the drain with my jasmine and orange scented body wash.

Besides, tomorrow is a new day. Maybe Declan will forget all about my little word mishap by morning.

Maybe.

Hopefully.

www.ingramcontent.com/pod-product-compliance
Lightning Source LLC
Chambersburg PA
CBHW031523310726
48971CB00008B/2334